HARD ROAD TO HOLFORD

The stagecoach run from Muddy Creek to Holford should have been an easy one. But when one of the passengers was being hunted by a Mexican revolutionary colonel who had been swindled in an arms deal, the trip was never going to be that simple . . . Forced to abandon their coach, the travellers had to experience many dangers before they could reach their destination . . . and even then their safety was by no means guaranteed.

GREG MITCHELL

HARD ROAD TO HOLFORD

Complete and Unabridged

LINFORD
Leicester

First published in Great Britain in 2011 by
Robert Hale Limited
London

First Linford Edition
published 2012
by arrangement with
Robert Hale Limited
London

British Library CIP Data

Mitchell, Greg, *1935* –
Hard road to Holford.- -
(Linford western library)
1. Western stories.
2. Large type books.
I. Title II. Series
823.9'2–dc23

ISBN 978–1–4448–1313–5

Published by
F. A. Thorpe (Publishing)
Anstey, Leicestershire

Set by Words & Graphics Ltd.
Anstey, Leicestershire
Printed and bound in Great Britain by
T. J. International Ltd., Padstow, Cornwall
This book is printed on acid-free paper

1

'Are you trying to kill us all?' Amos Risdon demanded.

The object of his wrath, a young stable hand standing nervously nearby was unsure of the crime he had committed but knew he was about to be told. The Rutherford Stage Coach Company's senior driver was known throughout the organization for his irascible behaviour early in the morning.

With a face as grim as the knocker on a morgue door, he asked again: 'Do you want to kill a whole coachload of people?' Then, without waiting for a reply, he stabbed an accusing finger at the rein buckled to the nearside leader's bit. 'The loose end of this rein fastening has not been put through the bottom part of the buckle. It can work loose. I've seen it happen. Damn lucky I always check. That jackass in the office

1

should be careful about who he hires. If I find this sort of sloppy work again, sonny, I'll see to it that you're out of a job. Now hold this horse till I tell you to let him go.'

Mumbling to himself, his weather-beaten face still flushed with anger, the driver continued checking the rein buckles on his team's bits. He was obsessive about that small detail. Once, after a team change, a rein had not been fastened properly and he had partially lost control of a very spirited pair of leaders. By sheer good luck the coach was not wrecked but from that day, twenty years ago, the coach driver trusted nobody and had always person-ally checked every rein buckle.

He paused in his task to see the new shotgun guard hurrying towards him. Unthinkingly he shook his head and scowled. He still did not know what to make of Chris Unwin. They had only done one previous trip together and a couple of vocal clashes proved that the young guard certainly had a mind of his own. The frown deepened when Amos saw what his companion on the box was carrying. What was the Rutherford Stage Line coming to?

Chris Unwin was as green as grass when it came to the coaching business. Not long from a border ranch, in Risdon's mind he lacked a few of the social graces that people seemed to expect from company employees. He was smart though, and would soon learn if his somewhat unconventional ways did not get him fired first.

Today was an example. As a guard he was expected to wear a six-shooter and carry a double-barrelled, 12-gauge shotgun, but lugging a Winchester carbine as well as the scattergun, he looked as though he was expecting a small war.

The driver completed his check, left the stable hands to hold the leaders and strolled back to where Unwin was stowing the carbine under his seat. 'What's all this about, young fella? I thought this company only supplied shotguns and I'm not real sure they would approve unauthorized firearms. What's the idea of the Winchester?'

Chris appeared to care little about the disapproval showing plainly on the older man's face. Deliberately he waited a second or two before replying, 'It's a bit of extra insurance I decided to bring along. Hasn't Hank told you yet?'

Hank was the company agent in the Muddy Creek office. He and the driver shared a mutual dislike of each other and conversed as little as possible. Rumour had it that they had fallen out years ago over the affections of the same woman, but the lady in question solved the problem by marrying someone else and moving away.

'If that fat little jackass had told me I wouldn't need to be asking you,' Amos replied. He glared in the direction of the office and grumbled, 'I'm in charge here and Hank should be telling me if trouble's expected.'

'He told me that there was a scare all along the border, something about Mexican bandits.'

Amos snorted. 'Hank should know better. This coach won't be worth robbing today. We don't have a big load of well-heeled customers and won't be carrying a strongbox until the run back from Holford. Given the way Hank flaps his mouth, the smarter road agents and even dumb Mex bandits would already know that. So let me in on the secret. What in the hell else is going on around here?'

'According to Hank, the army's been called out. There's a report that a big band of Mexicans has been chased over our border by government troops and they might try to resupply themselves by raiding ranches and robbing folks. But that ain't all. There's some Apache raiders also came out of the Sierra Madres. If reports are right, things could get mighty hot around here and there's little help to be had out on the road. Company rules or not, I'm bringing along a rifle in case we strike trouble.'

'Don't you reckon we have enough artillery?'

'A rifle might come in handy. The main problem with revolvers and shotguns is that they let any hold-up men get too close to the coach. That makes it easy to bring down a few horses and wreck it.'

The older man looked hard at the new guard. 'How many hold-ups have you ever been in, sonny?'

'Er — none but I've fought Indians and Mexican rustlers.'

'I've been stuck up twice and both times the hold-up men hid close to the road in easy shotgun range. Once they even shot the guard off the box. Make sure it don't happen to you. If trouble comes it will be close at hand and that shotgun will do a better job than a rifle. But don't go getting all heroic. If a bandit has you dead to rights, don't make a fight of it and risk lives to protect money. And if you get shot, try not to bleed all over the coach. Blood's hard to clean off.'

'I'll try to remember that,' Chris replied casually. 'But rules or no rules,

I'm taking this rifle. The horses won't notice the weight of an extra gun and I'll feel happier to have it handy if things go real bad.'

'Keep your voice down,' Amos hissed 'We don't want to scare the passengers. Let's get up on the box. Hank's about to load them aboard.'

The first passenger from the office was a pale, thin man wearing an expensive suit. He was in his late thirties with narrow hunched shoulders, and a worried, shifty look on a thin face dominated by a large beak of a nose and a pair of wire-framed spectacles. His main intention seemed to be to get aboard the coach as quickly as possible.

'Just our goldarned luck,' the driver said quietly. 'That's Larry Wilmot, claims he's a businessman but he's mostly into land speculation and a lot of deals that aren't as legal as they could be. He's a miserable sonofabitch who would skin a flea for its hide and then go looking for a market for the bones.'

'Our luck ain't all bad,' Chris said. 'Do you know the little honey coming next?'

The driver's usually solemn face relaxed as the pretty young girl with the brown hair and blue eyes looked up and smiled. 'It's a lovely day, Mr Risdon. Are you feeling well?'

'Sure am, Miss Fletcher.' Amos tipped his hat, allowed his face to break into a rare smile before saying softly to Chris, 'Don't get any ideas about that one. Most of the single fellas in town want to marry her and there's a few married ones who would consider murder, divorce, or even bigamy if they thought they could win her.'

The third passenger was an untidy individual with unkempt fair hair sticking out from beneath a battered, sweat-stained hat. His large soup-strainer moustache was tobacco-stained and it was several days since his chin had encountered a razor.

Amos allowed himself a little chuckle. 'That's Horace Weldon. It ain't too often he has the coach fare. I doubt that anyone around here would call him an upstanding citizen but there's lots worse about. He ain't too bad but some of our more respectable people think he's a blot on the landscape and sometimes he is. Folks who know him say he'd rob a bank but give away half if he thought someone needed the money more. Horace has seen the inside of a jail a time or two and he does not have a lot of respect for authority. He used to work in the buffalo camps but now does odd jobs and takes a great delight in annoying supposedly respectable people like Wilmot. My guess is that he must have fallen foul of the sheriff and is getting out of town until things cool down a bit. This could be a real interesting trip with that pair together.'

Another woman appeared, a small, stylishly dressed lady in her early forties. She too knew Amos and gave him a friendly wave before climbing into the coach.

The driver flashed his version of a welcoming smile. 'That's Maggie Cooper.

9

She's a widow, has a shop in town but visits her sister in Colorado about once a year when the weather is warm. She's a real nice lady.'

The last passenger was a broad-shouldered, dark-haired, young man with a neatly trimmed beard that almost hid a scar on his right cheek He was dressed in range clothes, and a cartridge belt and holstered gun showed under his rumpled brown coat.

'Don't know that one but he's a hard-looking critter,' Amos muttered. 'The name on the passenger list is John Jones. Sounds a bit suspicious to me but he could call himself George Washington as long as he has a ticket and behaves himself.'

Hank, the short, rotund company agent slammed the door behind Jones and called up to the driver. 'They're all aboard.'

Amos glared briefly at his old rival, took a firm grip on the reins and released the brake as the six-horse team started pawing impatiently and tossing their heads. 'Let 'em go,' he called to the men holding the leaders.

The eager horses jumped into their collars and the coach rocked slightly on its leather springs as it rolled forward.

On a hotel balcony overlooking the street, a man out of sight from those below waved his hat.

Out of the town, on a high ridge, two unshaven, travel-stained riders wearing Mexican sombreros were looking back towards the town. Both wore guns with the air of those who knew how to use them and their good horses seemed out of place with their poor clothing. The one watching through field glasses said to the other, 'That's the signal. He's on the coach. Colonel Dwyer will want to know. Let us get moving.'

They turned their horses' heads to the north and spurred away. The coach was moving at a good rate so they had to ride faster still but had greater ability to take rough short cuts. Dwyer liked to plan well in advance and the sooner the word reached him the sooner he could set his trap.

2

Conversation started to grow among the passengers as the miles rolled away beneath the coach's wheels. Wilmot started the words flowing with a burst of exaggerated courtesy toward the ladies, enquiring whether they were comfortable and could he help them in any way. They politely assured him that all was well and thanked him for his concern. Secretly though, Wilmot's false concern for their welfare grated on them. Both knew Horace Weldon only by repute but, unlike Wilmot, did not seem perturbed by his presence. He seemed to be remembering long-forgotten politeness and obviously was on his best behaviour.

Jones said enough to be polite but preferred to stay out of the small talk, speaking only when he was specifically addressed. He looked like a man with much on his mind and seemed more intent on studying the scenery.

Miss Fletcher revealed that her first name was Ellen and suggested that a first-name basis would make things less formal among the travellers. Weldon heartily agreed, although Wilmot would have preferred a slightly more formal atmosphere. He was at ease with the ladies but felt that Weldon and Jones were not his social equals.

Ellen saw Weldon fumble in his pockets, then he saw she was watching and, with a guilty expression, pulled his hand away.

'If you feel like smoking, Horace, I don't mind,' the girl said with a smile. She turned to the other woman. 'What about you, Maggie?'

The other laughed. 'I know what these men are like with their tobacco. Feel free to smoke if you like, otherwise you will all be nervous wrecks and snarling at each other by the end of this journey.'

Horace produced a plug of chewing tobacco. 'I don't smoke, I chew. There won't be any smoke to annoy you ladies, and I'll make sure I'm real careful when I spit out of the window.'

'That's a disgusting habit,' Wilmot said sharply. 'You shouldn't even mention it around respectable ladies.'

Horace was unrepentant. 'I don't see why not. I knew a saloon girl in Fort Worth used to chew. She was a real lady but could spit as far and as straight as most men. Yes sir, Judy was some girl.'

'I don't think these ladies are interested in your sordid relationships.'

'Hell — sorry ladies — she weren't no relation of mine.'

Wilmot assumed a haughty tone. 'Please consider the sensitivities of your fellow passengers, Horace. I hope that you won't regale us with stories of your more dubious exploits for the rest of the journey.'

Weldon just smiled and shrugged his shoulders. 'There's only one exploit I'm specially proud of, Larry my friend. I once threw a stuck-up jackass right off a coach.'

Wilmot understood the implied threat in the casual comment and fell silent. He too had heard of Weldon's chequered past.

In an attempt to lighten the atmosphere, Maggie changed the subject. 'Has anyone heard anything about those Mexican rebels who are supposed to have invaded us?'

Jones broke his silence and answered: 'I doubt it's an invasion. I had a ranch in Mexico for a while. The country has been in turmoil for years and every second bandit leader calls himself a general, or at least a colonel and, given the chance tries to take over the whole district. The Federales are inclined to be a bit ruthless with rebels and if any have come over our border it will be just to escape the army. They might steal the odd cow to eat or possibly take a horse or two, but then they'll get back across the Rio Grande as soon as possible. They don't want to add to their troubles by taking on our troops as well.'

'I was in Mexico recently.' Wilmot could not stay silent for long. 'I was looking into establishing hotels in Vera Cruz and Mexico City, but decided that the situation was too volatile for safe investment.' He neglected to mention that the Mexicans were not interested in the small amounts of money he was prepared to put up. Nor were they convinced that he was an honest man. Fast-talking entrepreneurs from all sources had, in their quest for easy money, descended on the strife-torn nation seeking to exploit legal loopholes and inexperienced or corrupt government administrators. But the Mexicans were becoming wiser and some enterprising 'businessmen' were currently residing in old Spanish dungeons in Mexico City. Wilmot had decided that money-making, even if slightly harder, was safer north of the border.

The coach rolled into the next change station, where the passengers were allowed to alight and stretch their legs while the teams were being changed.

Amos questioned Elmer Parry, the station operator, about the supposed Mexican invasion but the man had heard nothing. Nor had he heard of any Apache raiders, and he reacted nervously to the notion that they could be at large. These shadowy raiders could leave a broad swath of destruction behind them and only their victims would see them.

'So you ain't seen or heard anything to worry about?' Amos asked again. If trouble was about he wanted to know of it.

Parry wrinkled his forehead, thought for a while, then said, 'It could be nothing, but we saw two riders pass here about a quarter-hour before you arrived. They gave us a wide berth, which was unusual. I don't know what they were up to but they were riding hard and in no mood to socialize. My eyes are not that good these days but, going by their hats, they might have been Mexicans. If I was you I'd keep an eye open in case they try to hold you up along the way.'

17

'I'll do that. Much obliged, Elmer. Now I'll get these folks back on board.'

As the passengers climbed into the coach, the driver quietly told Chris, 'We might need to keep a sharp eye out. Those fellas Elmer saw were riding hard for a reason. Maybe I'm just old and suspicious but I think it could concern us.'

★　★　★

Miguel Dwyer was as comfortable as he could be seated on a blanket on soft grass with his back against the wool lining of a saddle, but the pain from his bandaged head prevented any real rest. He was young for a rebel leader; only in his late twenties, a handsome, charismatic figure with the right mixture of intelligence and daring that attracted men to his cause. As a leader he cared for the welfare of his men where he could. But his concern was not totally altruistic, for he knew that without them he was powerless. Some of those with him were newcomers to his cause, though a dependable few had worked for him on his ranch in more peaceful times. These few would obey him without question. Right or wrong, they would follow any of their young leader's orders. They needed no reason to rob or murder. Dwyer justified all his actions with a warped form of patriotic zeal. The good of the republic came before all else. If that coincided with his own advantages he felt obliged to pursue both aims at once.

The strongly built son of an Irish father and a Mexican mother, he had inherited his mother's dark hair but his skin was lighter than some of his relatives. He had also inherited a lifelong hatred for Americans, although he kept it carefully hidden when north of the border. Having been mainly educated in Texas he was completely at home on either side of the Rio Grande, but his loyalty would always be to Mexico.

Both his parents had been killed, his

father by the US Army and his mother by ill-disciplined government troops of the present regime. Because of the misdemeanours of the latter, Dwyer was dedicated to the task of removing the government from power and dreamed of the day when he would lead a rebel army into Mexico City. He had already raised a force of extremely efficient guerrillas and had made his presence felt in his own area by ruthlessly wiping out small military detachments. Buoyed by early success, he had given himself the title of colonel so that none would confuse him with a bandit. But then his fortunes had changed.

In a recent skirmish his careful planning had come to nothing. He had been unable to maintain the initiative when ammunition supplies failed at a crucial moment and a hasty retreat had become necessary. During his flight, his much-admired palomino stallion had been killed and he suffered concussion when it fell, just another disaster as his carefully laid plan unravelled. What should have been a victory had ended in a reversal and Dwyer blamed it on one gringo. That man's crime could not remain unpunished. Temporarily the colonel forgot his main objective and now was concentrating his efforts on apprehending the man who had ruined his plans and, worse still, had left him looking like a gullible fool. He dispersed his main force, crossed the border and sent out his spies. He would take the guilty one alive and he would die by inches. When that was accomplished he would return to Mexico and call together his scattered forces. Word of his vengeance would spread quickly and all would know then that Dwyer would deal swift and terrible retribution to those seeking to take advantage of him.

More than a score of heavily armed men had accompanied him and they, with their horses, were resting in the same shady grove. They little resembled any type of military force. Most were ragged, bearded and dirty and a couple sported bandages over minor wounds incurred in their latest clash with the army. The bandoleers they wore were half-empty too, although nearly all had supplemented their armouries with at least one revolver. The group had travelled far and fast and both men and horses looked close to exhaustion. All were hoping for a few hours rest but those hopes were dashed when they heard horses galloping towards them. The more anxious ones jumped to their feet and were reaching for weapons when a sentry called, 'Juan and Morino are coming.'

The two riders came pounding into the camp and halted their heaving mounts before their leader. The elder of the two, a wiry little man with a grey-streaked beard, gasped: 'He is on the coach. Thomas saw him and signalled from town.'

Juan, the speaker, had been Dwyer's *segundo* in their ranching days, a smart and thoroughly dependable man. He, like Thomas, was a great asset to the revolutionary's cause.

Thomas also had proved himself to be intelligent and reliable and the self-styled colonel trusted him implicitly. He was an Americano, a former Confederate who preferred not to live under a hated Yankee government. During the Civil War he had been in the Signal Corps and after the surrender, had retained the necessary tools to tap into telegraph wires. This skill had proved invaluable to Dwyer and he was happy to pay the embittered rebel handsomely for his services. He used just a single name and no one knew whether Thomas was his first or last name. Being fluent in both English and Spanish as well as Morse code, he had been able to intercept government signals and send false messages. It was he who had tapped out false warnings of a Mexican incursion that diverted American troops far to the eastern end of the border. A fake message about an Apache raid had also sent other soldiers on a wild-goose chase in Arizona, thereby enabling Dwyer to slip his men through the vacant area they had left. Because he kept his distance from Dwyer, he was not associated with the Mexican rebel and could wander around the American side of the border without attracting attention. It was he who had tracked down the man who had swindled Dwyer, a man calling himself Robert E. Grant.

'I want you to take four men, Juan. Get Grant off the coach and bring him here alive,' the leader instructed.

Juan, because of their long association, did not hesitate to speak his mind. 'Five men might not be enough, Miguel. We really need more than that to make sure that the plan works properly.'

Dwyer's head was paining and he was in no mood to argue. With an air of resignation he said, 'Take another man but that's enough. I can't wear out all my men on a job that a few can do — and look at the state of our horses.

Most will need feed and rest at least for today. Otherwise we might not get back over the border. Take the six fittest horses we have. Ride hard and intercept the coach. It can be on the trail or at a change station but get me that man.'

'What about the other people on the coach?'

Dwyer shrugged, then winced because the action hurt his sore head. 'I will leave that up to you. They are not important. Rob them if you like. Kill them if you have to but make it look like the work of bandits or Indians. I only want Grant. If they surrender and you decide that it is safe to spare them, just rob them, take the coach horses and leave them stranded. Remember though, they must think that you are bandits and not connected with any political activity. We do not want the United States Army to get involved here. I will leave the operation to you but you must bring that man to me alive. After that no one will dare to try cheating me again. Now select your men and horses and stop that coach.' Almost as an afterthought, Dwyer added: 'Take my cousin Francisco with you. He is keen to show what he can do. But keep an eye on him. He sometimes takes too many risks.'

'I will watch him,' the grizzled little man promised. 'It will be best if we strike the change station first to be sure that the coach cannot get past it. Then we will stop the coach before it gets to the station.'

Made short-tempered by throbbing inside his head, Dwyer said impatiently, 'I don't care what you do, Juan. Just bring that man to me.'

★ ★ ★

The coach was barely a mile short of the next change station when Chris sighted a dust cloud ahead, and in it the tiny figures of distant riders. This was not cattle country and these were unlikely to be cowhands, nor did travellers move in such groups unless danger was expected. He pointed. 'Looks like something odd up the trail a piece. I'm not sure those riders are friendly.'

'That makes two of us,' Amos growled. 'By the way they're spreading across the road they mean to stop us.'

'They look like Mexicans. What do you intend to do?'

'I sure as hell ain't stopping. I'm gonna try busting through them and reach the change station. We're not far from it. You shoot any sonofabitch that tries to stop us. Tell the passengers to get on the floor and keep away from the windows.'

'You don't think it's smarter just to stop and get robbed? What if the passengers get shot?'

'I'm in charge, I'll worry about that. Just tell them folks to keep their heads down and get to work with that Winchester.'

Chris leaned down and shouted to the passengers. 'There could be trouble ahead. We're trying to run through it.

Get on the floor and keep away from the windows.'

'What's happening?' Wilmot called but received no answer. The coach crew had other priorities. He would have liked to look out of the window but decided that it would be safer if he did not.

'Is it a hold-up?' Ellen asked. Her calm tone did not betray the anxiety she felt. She was carrying $600 to make the final payment on her family's ranch. It was the most money she had ever held in her life and it represented years of hard work on the part of her parents. To lose that would be a disaster. She wondered whether somehow the bandits had found out about the large sum she was carrying.

'I reckon there could be road agents ahead,' Jones told her. 'You ladies had best get on the floor because there's almost certain to be shooting if the coach is running through an ambush. Keep low because bullets will go through this coach like it was cardboard.'

Wilmot gave a terrified bleat and would have been first to hit the floor except that Horace caught him by the shoulder. 'Ladies first,' he said sternly.

'So much for my nice clean dress,' Maggie disguised her fear with an air of resignation as she slipped off the seat on to the dusty floor.

Ellen joined her there and Wilmot squeezed down on top of them.

'You're heavier than you look,' Maggie told him, 'but I'll forgive you if you are bullet-proof as well.'

'Won't be any bullets comin' down from above,' Horace muttered angrily.

Jones shook his head in disgust but realized that Wilmot would be a doubtful asset in possible fighting to come and refrained from any comment. Instead he drew a gun and stretched out on the seat near the window. Horace did likewise except that he covered the other side.

Chris produced his rifle. 'I'll fire a warning shot in the hope that they decide a hold-up might be too risky,' he told Amos.' If they try to stop us after that, they'll know that they're likely to get hurt.'

The driver shook the reins and called to his horses before replying, 'I don't care what you do as long as we can get this coach through to the change station. Try to keep them at a distance so they can't get easy shots at the team.'

The guard could not resist the opportunity. 'Do you still think I was wrong to bring this rifle?'

'I hope you can shoot as well as you talk,' Amos muttered.

Chris levered a cartridge into the rifle and fired a shot in the air, clear warning that the coach driver did not intend to be stopped. His worst fears were confirmed when the riders ahead started yelling like Indians and charged towards them. One of the strangers even fired an impossibly long shot with his revolver. It did no damage but confirmed the newcomers' hostile intent. At top speed the horsemen urged their mounts straight at the coach and the space between both parties diminished with frightening speed.

The guard opened a rapid fire in an attempt to keep the horsemen at a distance from the vulnerable team. It was difficult to hit moving targets from the top of a rolling coach but enough bullets passed close enough to worry the attackers. A couple veered off to the side, but one young Mexican on a buckskin horse spurred straight at the coach team. He fired first at Chris and his shot lodged between guard and driver. Then he emptied his six-gun at close range into the leading pair. His reckless attempt to stop the coach led him into making a fatal error and he was dangerously close on the guard's side as he turned his horse away to avoid being run down. Chris fired at him and the man flew backwards from his saddle. The coach wheels narrowly missed his rolling body as the vehicle sped toward its goal.

The other raiders started firing then and, unexpectedly coming up against rifle fire, they split, riding wide down both sides of the coach. Horace and Jones were taken by surprise and though they shot at the horsemen who flashed past the coach they did no damage. A couple of return shots tore through the coach body but missed those inside.

In a very short time travellers had passed through the bandits' cordon. The wild riders disappeared in the dust and, a hundred yards behind the coach, they began regrouping to make another attacking run.

Chris twisted around, partly kneeling on his seat as he waited for the Mexicans to appear through the dust cloud rolling in the vehicle's wake. For a brief moment he thought their luck was holding.

Then Amos hauled back on the reins, shouting: 'Whoa!'

The wheel horses sat back on their haunches and the coach began to slow.

Chris was concentrating on the riders who were quickly gaining on them but, between shots, called, 'Why are we slowing down?'

Amos yelled back: 'Because they shot our near-side leader and maybe the other one as well. The leaders are wobbling everywhere and are likely to go down in the next few yards. There'll be one hell of a crash — we could tip over if we don't stop. This team has no chance of lasting to the change station. We have to fight them here.'

'What about the passengers?'

'It's too late to hold a vote. Right or wrong, we're committed now, and they won't be taking prisoners. So shut your face and get that Winchester working.'

3

The coach stopped in a swirl of dust: it was just in time. The near-side leader collapsed and the off-side one was staggering. The swing and wheel horses became tangled in the traces and reins as they slewed sideways to avoid crashing into the stricken leaders, With his foot on the brake lever and a tangle of reins in one hand, Amos drew his revolver and waited for the attackers to come into range. Chris had emptied the magazine of his Winchester and snatched up the shotgun. A rider on a wiry black pony came charging up to the side of the coach until a charge of heavy buckshot blasted him from the saddle. The guard was looking about for another target when the four remaining attackers raced out of the dust, passed the coach and spurred their mounts out of range.

Horace and Amos snapped a few shots at them hoping to discourage further assaults. Jones was quickly reloading his gun after punching the fired shells from the cylinder. Wilmot tried to cower closer to the floor and was silently cursing the two women beneath him, who were preventing him from getting any lower.

'They're running,' Chris shouted. 'We've driven them off.'

Amos stopped surveying the wreckage of his team and, remembering his responsibility, called down, 'Is everyone all right?'

Maggie answered back in a nervous voice. 'I'm nearly crushed but nobody else looks injured.'

Jones jumped from the coach door, his revolver ready as he came. 'It looks like they have gone except for the one lying here near us. I'll just check that he's really out of the fight.'

'Be careful,' Horace warned. 'He could be playin' possum.'

Ellen looked out through a side

window and called to Amos, 'Are you and the guard all right, Mr Risdon?'

'We're both fine but keep your head down for a while yet, Miss Ellen. Those varmints might come back. I have a feeling that we haven't seen the last of them.'

Wilmot, now sure that the attackers were gone, was suddenly full of bravado. 'They won't try that again if they know what's good for them.' He produced a nickel-plated revolver from his pocket, made a great show of checking its cylinder, and slipped it back out of sight.

Jones looked over the dead Mexican in a manner that suggested he was familiar with such sights. He picked up the Remington 50/70 carbine lying nearby, blew a little of the dust off it and rolled back the breech block to see a live round in the firing chamber. Then he unbuckled the bandoleer slung over the dead man's shoulder. It contained roughly a dozen cartridges. Finally he removed a Navy Colt from the bandit's sash. It was fully loaded. 'At least we have a couple more guns now,' he told the others. 'I'll keep the carbine, but there's a spare six-shooter here. Does anyone need a gun.'

Wilmot was tempted to take it and try selling it later, but then he considered the remote possibility that the Mexicans might come back. If by some mischance he was captured and they found their late comrade's gun, it would not go well for him. He refused the offer, saying, 'I don't need it. I have one of my own in my side pocket.'

'Then why in the — ' Horace was about to let loose with some profanity when he saw the two women nearby. 'I mean, why didn't you use your gun when we were gettin' shot at?'

'There was no need. I was saving my shots in case you two needed someone to cover you while you reloaded.'

Horace suspected that Wilmot was too frightened to put himself in harm's way, but he was still on his best behaviour and did not express his opinion. Instead he went to help Amos untangle the two wounded leaders and remove their harness. Both were badly injured with no chance of recovery. Chris had taken up a vantage point lying flat on top of the coach, keeping watch with his rifle.

To everyone's surprise Ellen volunteered to take the spare gun if nobody else wanted it. Jones warned her to be careful as the weapon was loaded. She took it carefully, examined it briefly and put it away, first in the pocket of her skirt but, finding that awkward, later tucked it in her waistband instead.

Horace joked. 'You look downright bloodthirsty, young lady. Have you ever fired a revolver before?'

'I have not but I am prepared to learn in a hurry. I have seen them fired. What do you suggest?'

It was Jones who answered: 'Just cock it, hold it in both hands and let your target get good and close. Don't fire too soon.'

Horace looked at his fellow passenger

shrewdly. 'Sounds like you might be speakin' from experience, John.'

'I've shot a revolver a time or two,' the other replied. But the abrupt manner of his answer was a clear indication that Jones was not prepared to elaborate on his statement.

Amos decided that the coach could proceed with four horses. They would have to travel slowly because the swing horses were unused to leading, but the driver was confident that they could reach the change station. After loading the shot horses' harness on the coach he had one more task, a job that he hated. But it had to be done right, so the driver would not entrust the task to one of the others. 'Just get into the coach, ladies,' he said quietly. 'Don't look out of the windows because I have to shoot these wounded horses. It has to be done.'

'We know that,' Maggie said gently as she climbed back into the vehicle. She could see that Amos was feeling pretty miserable about the task he had set himself. The team had been a good one and, though he had driven many horses, the driver, for all his gruff ways, still felt for every animal in his care. Two shots and two clean kills later, a much subdued man punched the empty shells from his gun as he rejoined the others.

Maggie and Ellen climbed from the coach on the other side to avoid seeing the dead horses.

Wilmot would have boarded the vehicle again if Amos had not stopped him and explained, none too gently, that he wanted all to walk until he had tested the performance of his greatly reduced team. 'These horses have always been used to following leaders and are bound to feel a bit spooky. Some lose their confidence completely when they are forced to lead.'

The driver swung his team sideways to avoid the dead horses and they seemed to be responding well to their new positions. He even allowed himself a smile of relief. But it came too soon.

Watchers saw gun smoke erupt from a clump of greasewood about 200 paces away. The off-side leader went straight down and nearly dragged its team mate with it.

Chris fired at the bushes but had no real sight of the hidden shooter and had not adjusted his rifle sights for the range. A spurt of red dust just short of his target told him that he had missed. Another rifleman started shooting then and one of the wheel horses buckled under the impact of a bullet. Then the other leader went down. The coach was going nowhere.

Jones crouched behind a dead horse, the rifle to his shoulder, but could not see a target. 'Can you see who's shooting?' he called to Chris.

'Not a sign. But if anyone tries to make it across the open ground I should be able to get a good shot at them.'

'They won't be that dumb,' Amos muttered. He was seething with rage at the slaughter of his team.

Horace shepherded the two ladies behind the coach and Wilmot followed them.

'There's something odd about this,' Amos said as, with narrowed eyes, he sought the attackers. He had appropriated the shotgun although the current range was too great for such a weapon. 'I've never seen hold-up men hang around after the shooting started. They've lost two men already. The longer they stay, the greater the risk for them.'

'Unless they know there's hardly any risk,' Chris reminded him.

Wilmot decided it was safer under the coach where he was screened by a dead horse and from the safety of there ventured the opinion that the shooting would be heard at the change station. He was familiar with the route and seemed convinced that assistance would come from that direction.

The coach crew, however, were not so sure. The station staff was only two men who might fort up when they heard shooting. The travellers were not to know that Dwyer's men had already taken the precautionary measure of killing both company employees.

Now as they sheltered in an erosion gully, the remaining attackers were trying to find a way around their latest problem. They did not have the numbers to surround the coach and an attack across the open ground might not succeed.

Their wizened little leader scratched his grey-streaked beard as he studied the scene from behind the bushes on the gully's bank. Though he normally followed Dwyer's orders to the letter, he reached the conclusion that the plan had failed. Even worse, Francisco, Dwyer's cousin, had been the first one killed. The colonel would not like that. Reluctantly he ordered one of his men, 'Ride back to Colonel Dwyer. Tell him what has happened and that we have trapped the gringos, but we need more men to capture this Grant *hombre*.'

The man looked worried by the

prospect of bearing such bad news. 'What will I tell him about Francisco?'

'Tell him the truth. Francisco was brave but took too big a risk in riding so close to the shotgun guard. Hurry back with more men. I will keep these people here.'

The other was inclined to argue. 'They will escape, Juan. You do not have enough men to stop them.'

'That is where you are wrong, *muchacho*. To get help, they can only go forward or back. The gringos at the change station are dead and could not help them anyway. We can stop them going forward, and if they try to go back they will not get far on foot. With a few more men we can surround them. They really cannot escape. The colonel will be angry that we have failed here but he will know that we must make the best of the situation now. We can still make it work. Now, you must go.'

★ ★ ★

Amos risked a bullet to unharness the surviving horse and turn it loose. He could not use it and saw no purpose in getting it killed. Wilmot suggested that someone should use the animal to ride for help, although he excused himself personally on the grounds that he did not ride well. The others quickly vetoed that idea. A tired coach horse would be quickly run down by the Mexicans' ponies. The horse was reluctant to leave its dead companions and hung around until the driver shook his whip in its direction. Then, reluctantly, it trotted away.

Jones remained crouched behind a dead horse, carbine in hand and searching for a likely target. Horace kept low and ran in a half-crouch to where he was.

'Do you reckon they're still up ahead, John?'

Jones studied the apparently empty scene before him before replying cautiously, 'We have no reason to believe they're gone. There's something peculiar about this bunch. I don't think we are dealing with ordinary bandits. I think these are rebels. This carbine I have is Mexican cavalry issue and my guess is that it was taken off a dead soldier. The men out there could be army deserters but I have the feeling that they are one of the many guerrilla bands running around south of the border at present.'

'I wonder what they're doin' here, tryin' to stop coaches.'

'Damned if I know, Horace, but I reckon we'll soon find out.'

4

A siege situation developed with the stranded coach. The travellers kept under what cover there was except for Chris, who was lying flat on the coach roof looking for the first signs of another attack. His position was more uncomfortable than dangerous. He presented a small target and the besiegers were not inclined to waste ammunition. After a couple of unsuccessful tries they held their fire.

Amos had warned the passengers to keep out of sight and set an example himself by crawling under the coach where the dead horses offered some protection.

The afternoon sun beat down savagely and it was not long before the travellers found an additional problem. They had very little water. One large canteen of water was stored inside the coach for the use of the passengers and a smaller one was under the driver's seat for the pair on the box. The passengers' canteen was half-empty before Jones suggested that they ration what was left.

'We could still be here this time tomorrow,' the bearded man said, 'and if we are, we'll be mighty thirsty.'

Until then Maggie had been sure that the Mexicans would eventually abandon their attempted robbery. Now she asked in alarm, 'Are you saying that these bandits are not going to go away?'

'That's what I reckon, Maggie. There's something odd about this whole thing. I think we're all agreed that this is not an ordinary hold-up.'

'As someone who has never been held up before, I'll have to take your word for that.'

Ellen joined the discussion. 'It doesn't seem to make sense. They know they can't defeat us easily. There are not enough of them and they seem frightened to come too close. Why are they still hanging about?'

Jones continued: 'There are enough of them here to keep us in the one spot while someone brings up reinforcements. We have to consider the possibility that these characters could have friends in the vicinity.'

'If they had more they would have used them,' Amos said dismissively.

However his argument was far from convincing. The worried look on Horace's face showed unspoken agreement with Jones. Wilmot swallowed nervously and licked dry lips, He had slowly became aware of the gravity of the situation that confronted them. These bandits had no intention of riding away.

The heat eventually forced the guard off the roof and he was lying in the shade cast by the coach. Amos was sprawled nearby, sweating profusely and cursing under his breath as he brushed away flies. Ellen had joined them in a futile attempt to escape the heat inside the coach. She asked Chris, 'What do you think of our chances of getting out of this? I want an honest answer and promise not to scream or faint if the news is bad.'

'I don't know,' the guard replied. 'What do you think Amos?'

'They ain't going away and I reckon that when it gets dark they'll start working round the sides of us. We only have good cover from the front.'

Chris realized that the driver's opinion made a lot of sense. He studied the landscape around them. Their left side would be the more vulnerable. Clumps of low brush and cactus would screen anyone who kept low and approached carefully. The land sloped upwards gradually to a long sawtoothed range of mountains. An attacker on that side would be able to stay in carbine range and look down on their position when daylight came. Any outflanking movement would come from that direction. The eastern side was comparatively flat and open and attackers there would have little cover.

'As soon as it gets dark I'm moving out to the left because I reckon it won't be long before our bean-eating friends try coming in from that side,' the guard said to Amos. 'I'll leave you my Winchester and take the shotgun. It will be best for close-range work in the dark — too bad the company only supplied a few cartridges.'

'They don't expect fixes like the one we're in here. The gun either remains unfired or the problem is solved in the first couple of shots,' the driver explained. Amos was ever loyal to the company.

Ellen was failing miserably in her efforts to appear unconcerned. With a frown, she said, 'Are you sure that you should be away from the rest of us Chris? Wouldn't it be better if you took another of the men with you?'

'One man with the element of surprise should be enough to stop them creeping around the side of us. Their main attack might still come from the front and if that happens we will need every gun around the coach here. We know there are only four of them. If they lose another man, the odds will be very much in our favour and they might pull out.'

★ ★ ★

It was dusk when Dwyer heard the sentry challenge Juan's messenger. The self-styled colonel had been trying to doze but with his throbbing headache he was achieving little success. As befitted his mixed ancestry he swore in both English and Spanish when he heard of the situation. His mood was not improved by the knowledge that his cousin was dead and that Juan had been right. He should have sent more men. Reluctantly he ordered another six men with the fittest horses to join his lieutenant at the stranded coach. The horses had rested and grazed, so were a little better, but any extra travel would take its toll on them.

With the aid of one of his men,

Dwyer struggled to his feet. His speech was a little slurred as he had been sipping tequila in an attempt to get some rest, but his instructions were plain. Robert E. Grant was to be brought to him alive. The guard who had killed his cousin must also die. He did not care what happened to the others. A messenger was to report back to him as soon as the current situation was known. Once he had exacted his vengeance the colonel then had to slip his force back over the border. He was counting on Thomas to send enough confusing telegraph messages to lure the troops away from the area where he hoped to cross the Rio Grande. Another ordeal awaited him there, for his aunt Josefina would be shattered to learn of her only son's death. He cursed that man with the shotgun again. Miguel Dwyer would have his revenge.

After watching his men ride away, he called to the remainder, ordering them to be ready to ride at short notice. Though Dwyer hoped to remain at the present location for a while longer, he had no intention of being caught unprepared by some random cavalry patrol. He never rested his force without posting sentries, but in such broken country his enemies could come dangerously close without being detected.

★   ★   ★

The coach travellers had shared the last of the water, each taking a couple of swallows before passing on the canteen. Wilmot was careful to take only his rightful share. He had not changed his ways but Horace had taken him aside and threatened him with major injuries if he had persisted in his selfish behaviour.

Jones asked the driver, 'How far do you reckon we are from the next water?'

'The closest well is at the change station ahead, but there's some stirred-up *bandidos* between us and it, so unless our luck suddenly changes we won't be going there. The other change station is about twelve miles behind us but those Mexicans have horses. We would not have a chance of reaching there.' Then suddenly Amos seemed to have a flash of inspiration. 'I just remembered. There is a well — Halligan's Well — only about five miles away on the other side of those mountains. It is on the wagon road to the old Gopher Hill mine and there's an old trail to Holford runs off it.'

'Are there any people there who could help us?' Ellen asked.

'Not at the mine; it closed a couple of years ago, but there might be help at Halligan's. When there are Apache alerts the army sends out wagonloads of infantry and they picket the wells in the area. The aim is to deny the water to any raiders. They drop off a few men at each well and collect them later when the scare is over. As far as I know the army always pickets Halligan's when there is trouble. If we could get there, we would be fairly safe. Even if the soldiers aren't there we can at least get a drink and maybe someone could walk to Holford later to get help.'

'That would be a long, hard walk,' Horace said. He was familiar with the geography of the area.

Amos growled. 'We can worry about that later if we get to the well.'

'What are our chances of getting over the mountains?' Jones asked.

'They are pretty good. The slope will be tiring walking, and at my age I'm not looking forward to it, but it's not as if climbing is necessary. The ladies will find it hard and so will I, but with a few rests we should be able to make the crossing.'

'Shouldn't we stay with the coach?' Wilmot asked. 'Surely someone will come looking for us?'

'They might,' the driver agreed, 'but it could take days. It will be a while before the company realizes that we are stuck in the middle of the trip. Both ends of the run will think that the trip has been suspended because of the current scare. I don't like abandoning company equipment but there's no point staying with this coach.'

'I don't think we have any alternative,' Jones said. He looked at the mountains to the west. 'The sooner we get going after dark, the better.'

'If we are going mountain climbing,' Ellen said, 'Maggie and I had better change into more suitable clothes.' She turned to Chris. 'If you can get our bags from the boot, we can change in the coach. What will we need?'

'You'll need hats and whatever shoes or boots you can best walk in. Try to avoid wearing anything white if you can. It shows up too easily in the brush. You can take your reticules and money but nothing else.'

'I have a new dress that I haven't even worn yet,' Maggie protested. 'I don't like leaving that to some Mexican bandit.'

Horace laughed. 'I don't reckon those *hombres* will be too interested in it. Right now they would be more interested in stuff they could use.'

The thought of leaving his possessions behind also troubled Wilmot, because he was sure that the Mexicans would use the expensive clothing he was forced to leave. Tailors' bills were unpaid on some of his garments anyway so the financial loss was not as great as his fellow passengers imagined. Still, he was reluctant to abandon the best of his wardrobe. He made a couple of suggestions but the others were unyielding. Except for weapons all would carry only what could be distributed through various pockets and, in the ladies' case, their reticules.

The guard saw that the sun was sinking behind the mountains. He suggested that all prepare for the journey ahead and predicted that danger would probably come soon after darkness fell.

The travellers looked at the western mountains and wondered whether they would be lucky enough to see beyond them.

5

When the sun was down and the skyline lay silhouetted in the afterglow Amos and Chris discussed the direction of their retreat. Without pointing, in case they were observed, the driver showed the guard a small notch in the jagged skyline. 'That's where we should aim for. It's the shortest way over those hills and the climb is not too steep.'

'That's good. When you get there wait half an hour for me and if I don't show up by then, keep going.'

Amos frowned. 'Ain't you coming with us?'

'Not for a while. It's important that someone stays around here for a spell to give the impression that we are all still here. You are going to need a fair start with the passengers. I'll try to throw them off the scent. They can't track in the dark. Take my Winchester

59

and leave me the shotgun. It will be best for night work.'

'You think they'll attack tonight?'

'I'm sure of it,' Chris replied. 'Get the passengers away as soon as it's dark enough. I'll go out a way so that I intercept anyone who might be coming around the side under the hills. Otherwise they might run into you as you are leaving.'

'There are only three cartridges left for the shotgun. Will that be enough?'

'I don't intend starting a small war. It should be enough and I still have my six-gun. One way or another any fight will be over by the time I empty both guns.'

Ellen and Maggie announced that they were ready to travel but Amos warned them to stay in the coach until darkness fell. If unseen observers noted the change of clothing they might be alerted.

Dwyer's men had not fired for some time and the travellers were beginning to wonder whether they had left when a voice in heavily accented English called from somewhere in front of them. 'Can you hear me, gringos?'

The man had obviously taken advantage of the gloom and crept closer.

'I can hear you.' Amos peered into the darkness and shouted back.

'I talk for Colonel Miguel Dwyer. We want only one man. My colonel wants Robert E. Grant. If he surrenders the rest of you can go free.'

'You're barking up the wrong tree. We don't have anyone here by that name.'

'Don't lie to me. I know he is travelling with you. I am offering you your lives in exchange for one miserable, thieving sonofabitch. If he is not handed over you will all die when the colonel comes. This is your last chance.'

'I've heard of Dwyer,' Jones whispered. 'He was no colonel then but he had a big ranch about thirty miles south of mine. He was reckoned to be one tough *hombre*. He has no love for Anglos. The story is that his father was one of the San Patricios that General Harney hung in the Mexican War.'

The lanky driver studied the group for a moment, then said, 'I suppose one of you gents is that Grant character? The name is obviously a false one.'

The three male passengers looked suspiciously at each other and each denied that he was the person in question. Horace and Wilmot were well-known but Jones was a stranger to all.

'Looks like we've been mistaken for someone else,' Horace said quietly.

'I wonder why Dwyer is after this character?' Jones looked puzzled as he spoke.

Wilmot was about to make a statement but could only utter a feeble croak. Fear had made his voice too shaky.

'You have the wrong people,' Amos called back. 'There's no Grant with us.'

'There is and we know it. Don't waste your lives for a miserable thief.'

Chris whispered to the driver. 'Get

everyone moving. While that character's keeping us talking, one of his friends could be working around us for a better shot. I'm going out to the side to cover you as you move out but I won't shoot unless I have to. Fire a shot in that *hombre*'s general direction if he calls again. He'll see the muzzle flash and think we are still all at the coach. When you do that, get moving. I'll catch you up.'

'Gringo — what is your answer?'

Amos fired back although he knew that his chances of scoring a hit were minimal.

No shots came back in reply.

Then they moved out silently in single file with the driver leading and Jones the last in the line.

Chris stole quietly closer to the besiegers to cover the others as they crept away behind him. He was about fifty yards from the coach when he found a clump of boulders that offered both protection and deep shadows in which to hide. There he waited.

Faint sounds came to him as his companions groped their way up the slope in the dark. He knew that on such a still night the sounds would carry, and he hoped that none of their attackers was nearby. His heart sank when he heard a small sound as though a boot had slipped on loose gravel. The origin of the sound was not far away.

Any doubts that enemies were abroad were quickly dispelled when he heard two voices conversing in low tones in Spanish. The hunters had heard the travellers making their way up the hill and were satisfied that their quarry was some distance away. They felt it was safe to speak.

Chris peered into the gloom, trying to catch the first glimpse of movement and hoping that his adversaries would stay together. He knew there had been four men barring their way. One was out somewhere in front of the coach. Unaware that one had returned to the colonel's camp, the guard estimated that he could be facing three men. With the spare cartridge held between the fingers of his left hand, he cocked both hammers and watched for his first target.

A vague shape appeared in the gloom about twenty yards away. It moved like a man and Chris knew that no friends would be coming from that direction. Aiming as best he could in the darkness, he squeezed the trigger. The gun recoiled solidly against his shoulder but he knew he had scored a hit. Where were the others?

A rifle crashed like a cannon shot and a long streak of red flame stabbed at him. The shooter was firing at the shotgun's muzzle flash but failed to score a hit. Instinctively Chris fired the second barrel. Immediately he broke the gun, slipped in the remaining cartridge and listened. There was hoarse breathing and he caught the sound of nearby movement on the ground. Uncertain as to the condition of the noisy one, he fired again quickly and all sound and movement ceased.

If there was a third man he would have undoubtedly joined in the fray so the guard took a calculated risk.

With little time to waste, he discarded the empty shotgun and ran across to where his closest victim lay. Any extra firearm that the travellers could acquire could be well worth the risk taken to collect it. Hurrying to his second victim, he groped about in the darkness. Seconds passed like hours because, for all he knew, a third man might already have been stalking him. Then his boot kicked a fallen carbine and, with great relief, he snatched it up. It was the work of a moment to unbuckle the bandoleer over the dead man's shoulder and make a hasty retreat. He had been lucky and knew it. With two opponents fewer and another carbine and ammunition he set off to find the others.

He had not gone far when he heard another more distant sound: the trampling of horses. The attackers had been reinforced. Shouts came then as the newcomers called to their dead comrades. Chris could only hope that the nearby hills might have made the shots echo, disguising where the shooters had been. Likewise, the brush could have obscured the muzzle flashes from the sight of the other attackers, but he could not be sure. If the Mexicans suspected that the travellers were climbing the mountains they would soon catch up with them on horseback.

From the captured bandoleer the guard reloaded the carbine and crept further up the hill. He paused a while to catch his breath and listen for the sounds rising from the plain below.

A short while later he heard names being called repeatedly, as though the new arrivals were trying to locate the two men he had killed. This did not persist for long however, as the continuing silence confirmed the belief that both were dead. Then he heard the clatter of shod hoofs on rock. Riders were coming in his direction.

The hillside where Chris stood was

fairly open and even in the dark movement or a slight sound would be noticed by the approaching horses. It was safest to sink down on the ground where he was and lie motionless. This gave him the best chance of remaining undetected but, in the event of his being discovered, he would have the advantage of surprise. Stretched on the stony ground with his hat brim concealing his face and his body covering the straight lines of the rifle barrel, the guard waited.

Through the gloom he could just discern two riders, their horses moving at a walk about ten yards apart. They had already passed where he had killed the men but in the darkness had not seen the bodies.

Scarcely daring to breathe he listened as the sounds came nearer. It seemed that the closest rider must discover him although his companion was much lower on the slope. He was contemplating his chances of killing the nearest man and seizing his horse when the terrain came to his aid.

The man's horse stumbled into a small ditch. The rider swore softly in Spanish and allowed the horse to pick its own footing on the unseen ground. The animal turned slightly downhill and moved away from the course that would have taken it straight to Chris. The rider, alert now for another possible stumble, took little notice of anything else until he was past where the guard was lying.

Suddenly one man called to the other, which drew the hidden guard's attention to another sound. The beating of hoofs came from the plain below. The others in the group were charging the coach and hoping that the darkness would protect them until they were nearly upon the defenders. The riders who had bypassed Chris also turned their mounts downhill. He watched them fade into the darkness, wondering whether they were working to some prearranged plan or had abandoned their search in their eagerness to plunder the coach.

A few shots came from the scattered riders, but all shooting ceased as the Mexicans realized that they had charged an empty position.

Even in the darkness Chris could see dust swirling as the riders reined in. Then the shouting started as they realized that their intended victims were no longer there.

Confident that the men on the plain would neither see nor hear him, Chris began climbing the long slope towards the notch on the skyline. It was pointless attempting to conceal tracks. Dwyer's men would find them. In a few minutes, or at most a few hours, the hunters would be on their trail.

6

The long steady climb had taken its toll on the party from the coach, forcing them to take frequent rests, but fear dictated that the rests were short ones. They had heard the commotion behind them and at any time expected to see their hunters come charging up the mountain in pursuit.

Concern was felt for Chris too, but Jones was quick to point out that the last shot that they had heard had been from a shotgun. The guard had fired three shots and his opponents only one. 'I reckon he'll be along soon,' the bearded man said.

'He could still have been wounded,' Maggie argued.

'One of those Mexes might have finished him with a knife,' Wilmot told them. 'That way we wouldn't hear a sound. They are bad people with knives.'

Amos disagreed. 'He wouldn't be so careless as to let a man get close to him with a knife.'

'Maybe he threw it,' Wilmot suggested.

'I've seen the odd knife-fight,' Horace told them, 'and nobody in his right mind throws a knife. There are mighty long odds against a man gettin' killed by a thrown knife.'

Jones agreed. 'That's right. I think we'll find that Chris has had to lie low until those riders are well out of the way.'

'We should know soon enough,' Amos said. 'It sounds like those road agents or rebels or whatever are going back down the road thinking we've turned back. It will be daylight before they discover that we went in a different direction and it could be a while before they pick up our tracks. We have a couple of hours' start on them.'

Wilmot still feared waiting around. 'We should be going. We have two women to protect.'

'Don't worry about us, Larry,' Ellen told him. 'I think it is important that we all get together again before setting off. I don't mind waiting for Chris. We owe him that. He has looked after us well so far.'

'But he's young and fit and can soon catch up. If the bandits can follow our tracks, Chris can follow them too.'

Horace growled. 'He can't follow them at night. Now we wait here for him until the time he agreed on runs out. We don't just leave him. Do you understand me?'

Wilmot nodded.

★ ★ ★

Dwyer had slipped into an uncomfortable, alcohol-induced sleep a short while before the messenger from Juan's men arrived. When his men wakened him, he rolled on to the sore side of his head and treated them to a burst of ill-tempered profanity. The messenger's tidings did nothing to improve his mood. 'They have escaped, you tell me? Escaped to where?'

'We do not know, Colonel. Juan said that we would soon find them in the morning because they are on foot. He has also collected the horses from the change station, so we have a few fresh mounts.'

'Coach horses,' Dwyer said disdainfully, 'half of them not broken to saddle and the rest not used to carrying riders. With a stage station wiped out and a coach overdue, how much time does Juan think we have before the army gets on our trail?'

'He did not say,' the man replied fearfully.

With an air of resignation the leader muttered: 'Get all the others together and saddle a horse for me. We will join Juan and then see what we can do about this situation.'

As he nursed his aching head and fought down nausea, Dwyer thought how seriously one man had affected his ambitions. People were joining his force and he had hoped that it would swell into a revolutionary army. However, his last clash with government troops had been a débacle but not through lack of planning on his part. He could lay the blame directly at the door of this man, Grant. His dishonest dealings had robbed him of victory and Dwyer meant to get the culprit if he had to follow him to Canada. Grant had duped him and few people will follow a fool. To recover his reputation, he had to capture Grant and make such a terrifying example of him that none would dare cheat Miguel Dwyer again. Francisco's death was a further incentive to leave no survivors among those who had caused it.

The revolutionaries were skilled in the art of breaking camp and moving quickly. Their survival depended upon it. In a short while they were ready to ride. Two men offered to help their leader into the saddle but he angrily waved them aside. Settling in the saddle, he waved his arm and the cavalcade turned their mounts towards the stage road, which lay several miles to the east. It would be an uncomfortable ride but Dwyer was intent on regaining the initiative.

★　★　★

Chris found the hill climb steeper than he had imagined and stopped frequently to catch his breath. At each pause he stood listening. The hoofbeats had faded into the distance and he was sure that the horsemen had followed the wrong trail. He hoped they would not come back but logic told him that they would.

The ascent was making him dry, the upward slope seemed endless and the knowledge that it would be a long time before he reached water was beginning to worry him. He wondered too if the women were feeling the strain of their long, uphill walk. It seemed ages before he grew close to the rendezvous place. His legs were aching and he was about to rest again when he heard Amos's menacing growl. 'That had better be you, Chris.'

'It's me. Don't shoot.'

The tall driver stood up from behind the boulder that had concealed him. 'What happened back there?'

'There were two of them. I got them both but a lot of others have arrived. We just got away in time. How are the others?'

'The ladies were feeling the climb a bit but there's not a word of complaint from either of them. They've had a chance to rest for a while now but the downhill journey will still be hard on them. I think we'll all be stiff and sore tomorrow. Jones ain't saying much. Wilmot's complaining that his new boots are hurting him and Horace is inventing new ways to stir him up. They're just over the crest from us. I thought it safest if we didn't stop on the skyline. We all got in a lather of sweat climbing this danged mountain and now our clothes are damp and it's cold.

The sooner we get moving again, the better.'

'Just before we join the others — that colonel, or whatever he is, seems mighty keen to catch up with that Robert E. Grant character. That's a fake name if ever I heard one. Do you reckon it's one of our passengers?'

'Could be,' the driver admitted. 'Wilmot has been south of the border, and where money is concerned he would sell his own mother. Jones admits to living in the same general area as this Dwyer character and his name seems more like an alias. He could be our man. Then again, Horace has been in his share of shady deals in the past. But as far as I know, he has not been in Mexico recently. That colonel probably knew that he was dealing with a crook but did not worry about the false name until he found he had been swindled somehow. I'd dearly love to know what got him so riled up.'

'I suppose it doesn't really matter now,' Chris said. 'We have killed four of his men and it has probably become a matter of revenge. If the leader lets us get away, he might lose the respect of some of his followers. I reckon they'll be on our tracks at daylight.'

The others greeted Chris enthusiastically. They were already thirsty and keen to begin their journey to Halligan's Well. When pressed for details of the shooting they had heard, he said quickly that he would explain later. It was more important that they should start their journey again.

The guard claimed back his Winchester and offered Amos the carbine and bandoleer that he had taken. The driver declined and suggested that the weapon should go to one of the younger men. Horace immediately passed the Remington and its ammunition to Wilmot.

'Just what you need, Larry,' he said with mock enthusiasm. 'I'm sure you're a better rifle shot than me. Be careful though, it's probably loaded.'

'It is,' the guard affirmed.

Wilmot had fired a small-calibre rifle

a few times and took the carbine gladly. His previous misgivings about using a captured weapon were now gone. He would feel safer with it, and if he survived he might be able to sell it later.

Amos was the only one who knew the location of the well, so he took the lead as they started down the hill. The walking was slightly easier but the steep ground still put a strain on the travellers' knees. The darkness and the slope also made it hard for people to see where they were going.

Horace linked arms with Maggie and Chris held Ellen's elbow. Both women were hampered by their long skirts and needed assistance.

Amos was the first to fall. Some loose rocks rolled from under his feet and he fell flat on his back. He was calling down the wrath of Heaven on the landscape and might even have called for help from Hell if he had not remembered that there were ladies present.

Horace gave him little sympathy and

chuckled. 'We ain't never gonna get down this hill if you start lyin' down on us, Amos. But then, while you're down there, you might try rollin' to the bottom.'

The driver's angry reply was cut short by a crashing gun shot from close at hand.

7

Six pairs of startled eyes swung towards the sound. The smell of burnt powder hung in the air and even in the poor light a cloud of gun smoke could be seen hovering around Wilmot.

'I'm sorry,' he said weakly. 'I slipped and the gun went off. I think the hammer got caught on my coat.'

'Lucky someone didn't get shot,' Amos growled. 'Don't reload that damn thing.'

'It sounded like a cannon,' Jones said.

Horace suggested, 'It was probably the short barrel. Some of them carbines have a mighty loud bark.'

'Unfortunately it was loud enough for our Mexican friends to hear if any are still hanging about the coach,' Chris reminded them.

With that thought in mind the party made all haste away from the scene.

'I was meaning to ask you,' Ellen said to Chris as he helped her over a rough patch of rock. 'Who were the San Patricios that John mentioned earlier?'

'Depending upon your point of view,' the guard replied, 'they were either cowardly deserters or heroes. They were mostly Irishmen who deserted from our army in the Mexican War and swapped sides because they did not approve of the invasion of Mexico and the way that the war was being fought. They put up a helluva fight for the Mexicans who saw them as heroes. Eventually they were killed or captured and most of those captured were hanged. Dwyer's old man was probably among them.'

'It seems to me that they deserved it, turning against their own friends. We were only bringing freedom to Mexico.'

'That's not the way the Mexicans saw it. There were American officers too, who doubted the justice of that war, and the way some of our troops behaved did not win too many Mexican hearts. I've lived on the border long enough to know that there are two sides to every story. I don't pretend to know all the rights and wrongs but have heard stories from men who were there and reckon things could have been done a lot better.'

Ellen laughed softly. 'I didn't think there was such a serious side to you, Chris.'

'Well don't laugh too much because if you fall over and break a leg I might have to shoot you.'

They continued the descent, stumbling and sliding but finding it marginally easier than the uphill side had been. The guard stayed close to Ellen, enjoying her warm, gentle company after the harshness of the previous day's events.

★　★　★

Dwyer had not heard the shot. He had been sleeping on the seat of the empty coach while waiting for his men to reassemble. When one of his followers woke him, he muttered angrily, 'What is it?'

'It was a shot, Colonel. It came from the top of the mountains. It sounded like one of those Remington guns.'

'It could be our missing men. How many shots did you hear?'

'It was only one shot. Our men had no need to climb that mountain on foot. Their horses were not far away. We know that the gringos have one of our rifles. I think it was them.'

Dwyer settled back on the seat. 'They won't get far on foot. As soon as it is light we will start tracking. Pass the word. All men must be ready to move by dawn. Now call me again just before it is light.'

★ ★ ★

Corporal Ignatious Quinn was similarly unimpressed when the sentry called him. 'What is it, Ridley?'

'I heard a shot, Corporal. It came from up on the mountain.'

The big corporal threw aside his blankets and started pulling on his boots. He knew that Ridley was an experienced man whose judgement he had learned to respect. 'Wake the others,' he ordered. 'But tell them to be quiet.'

Five other soldiers were scattered around the camp. Three were in a roofless adobe ruin and two more were sleeping in the ruins of an old stake corral that had been reinforced by a number of conveniently placed boulders and a few packs. Both sites overlooked an old well surrounded by a low, crumbling, stone wall. They had been dropped there from a wagon the previous afternoon. At the time they felt that it would be a pleasant break away from the discipline of the army post. There had been similar scares before but Apaches and lawbreakers steered clear of guarded wells and being on water guard had never presented any dangerous situations in the past.

Hinkler, the newest recruit, asked in a thick German accent, 'Is it Apaches, Corporal?'

'How the hell would I know? One thing is sure, though. People don't normally walk round this country in the dead of night unless they're up to no good. Now load your rifle and keep under cover. Don't attract attention to yourself by moving about — and keep a sharp eye out.'

For half an hour the little force remained alert with their long infantry Springfields ready for immediate action, but no threat materialized. However, the corporal took no chances and arranged a system of guard rosters where a couple of men at a time could snatch a bit more sleep.

Those who remained on guard had heard fearsome stories of night-raiding Apaches and needed little incentive to stay awake. The calls of night birds and the rustling of leaves in the nearby brush only added to the soldiers' anxiety.

The coach travellers were not far away but thirst was making every yard seem like a mile. They reached the wagon road on the valley floor just as dawn was breaking. For a couple of minutes they sat and rested, but all were anxious to reach the water as quickly as possible.

Chris asked Amos, 'Which way to the well?'

The driver assumed a puzzled look and shook his head. 'I don't rightly know. I haven't been here for years. We could be north or south of it . . . We can't afford to go in the wrong direction. Them ladies are looking mighty weary and I don't mind admitting that I am feeling it too.'

The guard looked to the north where the trail disappeared over a slight rise. In the gradually improving light they could see a fair distance to the south and saw no sign of the ruins said to be near the well. 'If everyone waits here, I'll go to that rise and see what I can see,' he told the others. 'There's no point in everyone going if we have to retrace our steps later. If you see me wave my hat, come and join me.'

The others were pleased to rest for a while and offered no argument, so Chris left his Winchester with Amos and set out along the road. The light was gradually improving and the road was better than the steep hillside, making walking much easier. He was almost at the rise when it became light enough to see the tracks of a wagon and team on the trail. It had gone north and then come back south over its own tracks. Things were starting to look hopeful and they looked even better from the top of the rise. A quarter of a mile ahead the guard saw some adobe ruins and an old stake corral. Figures were moving about and he glimpsed a blue uniform. Elated, he waved his hat to the others.

'There are soldiers camped further down the road,' he said when they arrived. 'In a few more minutes we'll all be able to have a drink.'

'Even water is going to taste good,' Horace said enthusiastically as he looked towards the distant well.

As though revived by the sight, the party straggled off towards the camp. Maggie was a little behind the others as she had been emptying a stone from her shoe and Chris waited for her as she replaced the shoe and stood up. By chance she glanced up the hill they had descended and said urgently, 'Chris, there's someone on top of the hill. I just saw the sun flash on metal.'

The guard looked up. At first he saw nothing, then he caught sight of a movement. The newly risen sun revealed a group of riders on the mountain top. Catching the woman by the arm, he started to run after the others. When Wilmot looked back at them he shouted, 'I can see riders on the mountain. They'll be here soon. Run.'

Having been given a warning, Wilmot set an example, taking off like a startled hare and shouting as he passed the others, 'Run. They're here!'

Jones waited until Maggie and Chris caught up. By this time the horsemen were plainly visible because of the dust they raised as they forced their horses down the steep slope. As soon as Maggie had hurried past, he said to Chris, 'How long do you think we have before they get here?'

'Could be as little as five minutes, I reckon. We might just get to those soldiers ahead of them but it's going to be very close. We don't have the fire power to stop that many. There's a chance we could delay them but we won't stop them. Our only hope is to get within range of those soldiers at the well,' the guard said. 'They could give us covering fire. Their long-range rifles will reach nearly a mile.'

Jones did not agree. 'They might reach that far but most of those soldiers can't shoot for sour apples. Uncle Sam does not believe in target practice. The army is happy as long as the soldier keeps his rifle clean and can drill properly with it. We can only hope that they have a couple of veterans who have swapped lead a few times before.'

The two men deliberately lagged

behind but only one person showed concern about them. Occasionally Ellen glanced back to see where they were. The others were more intent on reaching safety, but those few backward glances put the girl high in Chris's estimation. She was worried about the whole group, not just her own personal safety. 'Come on, hurry,' she called urgently to the rearmost pair.

'We're coming,' Chris shouted back. 'Don't wait for us — keep going. Get to those soldiers as quick as you can.'

'If they could all run like Wilmot,' Jones observed, 'you and I would not have to wait behind here to slow those riders down. He sure can run but I'll give him a bit of competition when those people reach the soldiers. I don't intend being back here one second longer than I need to.'

★　★　★

'Corporal,' called Hinkler as he pointed. 'Look down the road.'

Quinn looked in the direction the soldier indicated and saw a most unexpected sight. One civilian with a rifle in his hand was sprinting towards the camp. About a hundred yards behind him two men and two women were hurrying along, while a further hundred or so yards behind them two men with rifles were walking at a much slower pace, halting occasionally and looking back.

'Take up your positions and make sure your rifles are loaded,' the corporal ordered. 'There's something funny going on. Nobody is to shoot without my order.'

A soldier called: 'Who do we shoot? Are those men behind chasing the ones in front?'

'Them women ain't likely to be charging against us,' another man observed. 'Like Quinn said, we don't shoot until we know what the hell is happening here.'

'Shut your ugly faces,' Quinn snapped. 'That man in front is yelling out something.'

Almost out of breath and running now on sheer adrenalin, Wilmot was trying to call a warning but could only utter a croak between breaths.

The corporal listened for a couple of seconds. 'He's yelling something about killers — must be Apaches.' He called to his men: 'Set your sights at five hundred yards and be ready to fire at anyone coming over that rise. But wait for my orders.'

★ ★ ★

'Wilmot's nearly at the army camp,' Jones told Chris. 'The others will be there in a minute or two.'

'So will our Mexican friends. They're on the trail now and are going to cover the ground mighty fast. Let's get as close to the soldiers as we can and hope that someone there has sense enough to give us a bit of covering fire. You and I can't make it all the way to the camp before we get caught up in a fight.'

The two men ran another hundred

yards and stopped again. Men panting for breath don't shoot very well. They saw the others straggling into the army post but the thunder of hoofbeats rising from the road behind the hill told them that they had no chance of outrunning the riders.

With no other option they took up a position among some boulders at the side of the trail. The noise of galloping horses grew closer at every second.

Jones checked the sights' on his carbine. With so few cartridges, he could not afford to waste shots. Training the weapon on the crest of the hill he said quietly, 'I reckon things are just about to get awful busy around here.'

8

Suddenly, as if they had sprung from the ground, riders surged over the crest. Being unfamiliar with the country and confident that their intended victims could not outrun them, they halted briefly to survey the scene. It was not what they expected. They saw people running into the ruined hut and then smoke erupted from the ruin's windows and the stake corral. Bullets hummed overhead or kicked up dirt in front of them as the sound of the shots came a fraction of a second later. While the riders milled about in confusion, Juan called to Dwyer. 'There are soldiers there. We should get back behind the hill.'

Not far away, the coach guard found his target. The sunlight was flashing on the central horseman's silver spurs and silver-decorated sombrero as he wheeled his mount around and shouted orders to his followers. That he was the leader of the group was obvious. Put him out of action and the situation could alter greatly. The moving horse brought the target briefly into the Winchester's sights and Chris opened fire. The shot almost missed but nicked Dwyer's right ear as it punched through the brim of the hat.

The colonel stifled a shocked cry but turned a shade paler when he realized how close he had come to being killed. With blood trickling down the side of his head, he shouted, 'Down there — in those rocks. Kill those two men.'

Jones fired and the man near Dwyer grunted, dropped his rifle and clutched at his saddle horn.

Other shots were kicking up dust around the horsemen or buzzing uncomfortably close. They were landing around the area randomly, the accuracy of aim depending upon the skill of the individual shooters, but Dwyer could see that it would not be long before men and horses were hit. He could not afford more casualties. 'Get back over the hill and dismount,' he ordered. As he spoke he pulled his mount around and a nudge from his silver spurs sent it racing back the way they had come.

'They're running,' Wilmot had recovered his breath enough to shout. Then, in what he considered would be an impressive contribution to the battle, he loosed a shot after the departing riders. He never knew where the bullet went but the loosely held rifle butt slammed into his shoulder so hard that the nail of his right thumb peeled a piece of skin from his upper lip. At the same time the roar of the short-barrelled carbine set his ears ringing.

'What the hell was that?' a soldier cried.

'None of your business — keep firing,' Quinn bellowed back.

Chris was pleased to see the revolutionaries retreat but guessed what they were planning. He nudged Jones. 'Let's make a run for it before those *hombres* come back on foot. They're only putting their horses somewhere safe.'

Hoping that the soldiers would keep their fire high, the pair left cover and sprinted towards the ruins. A few shots flew overhead but more disconcerting were shots that came from behind as Dwyer's men formed a firing line along the top of the rise. Already a couple of bullets had missed by not much.

As the pair neared the army camp a man with the two light blue chevrons of an infantry corporal on his sleeve appeared from behind the ruined building. 'Get behind the house,' he shouted.

Chris and Jones were happy to oblige and eagerly sought cover as they gulped air back into their lungs.

Then Ellen appeared, holding a soldier's water canteen in her hand. A pleasant sight at any time to the parched, exhausted shotgun guard, she looked like an angel. The water was tepid and did not taste the best but Chris thought it was the most delicious drink he had ever tried. It took a great effort of will to take only a couple of swallows and pass it on to Jones.

'Thanks, Ellen,' he gasped. He would have liked to say more but was still trying to catch his breath.

Jones added his thanks but any further conversation was forgotten as a bullet whined off the top of the adobe wall that sheltered them. All three instinctively ducked.

Then suddenly the shooting stopped.

Private Ridley had built himself a small barrier of stones behind a narrow gap in the stakes of the corral. He had a good field of fire and eagerly sought a target on the distant ridge line. There was movement but it was too quick and distant to risk a long-range shot. 'They're still there,' he called to Quinn. 'I think they're trying to Injun up on us.'

The corporal looked puzzled. He turned to the new arrivals. 'Can anyone tell me what's happening around here?'

Making sure that he kept below the level of the adobe wall, Amos told him,

'We are all from a coach that was going to Holford from Muddy Creek. We were jumped by a gang of Mexicans. They killed our team and I think they have probably wiped out one of the coach line's change stations. We were cut off from water so we hiked over the mountain to this well. We've been in a running fight with them since yesterday.'

'Have you lost any people?'

'Not so far but we have been lucky.'

'I've never heard of bandits chasing folks like this,' Quinn said. 'This sounds like more than a robbery.'

Chris joined the conversation. 'Those riders out there are a bunch of Mexican revolutionaries. They are after a character named Robert E. Grant who swindled their leader somehow. They thought he was on the stage and won't believe otherwise.'

The corporal looked sharply at the two coachmen. 'Are you sure he is not with you? Folks out here use all sorts of names when it suits them.'

Amos shook his head and spoke softly so that the others would not hear. 'We only have three male passengers, Wilmot and Horace Weldon are well-known around Muddy Creek. The only real stranger is John Jones and since yesterday he has proved himself to be a very useful *hombre*.'

Quinn frowned. 'That name sounds like a fake to me,' he said, 'Sounds about as real as Robert E. Grant.'

Another bullet struck the top of the wall nearby and a couple of the soldiers fired back.

'They're trying to work around us,' one soldier called.

'Get those people inside the walls,' Quinn ordered.

'I have a repeater and we have two carbines as well,' Chris told him. 'Where do you want me?'

'Cover the doorway or one of the windows. Those carbines won't be much use. I saw the way that passenger of yours got kicked when he fired one. Anyone firing those guns will go gun-shy after the first shot. Where did you get them?'

'We took them off dead bandits,' Chris replied.

The corporal laughed. 'I thought a few of those Mexican shots sounded a bit too loud. They have the wrong ammunition. They are using rifle cartridges with the full seventy grains of powder, intended for firing in a rifle weighing about ten pounds. The carbine round has a lighter bullet and a lot less powder. In a seven-pound cavalry carbine, the heavy infantry load goes off like a cannon. The carbine can handle the full load but sure as hell, the shooter suffers. Both cartridges look the same but carbine shells have a bit of dye around the priming caps to show the reduced load. When you get all those coach folks inside the walls, check the ammunition they have. Use those rifle rounds only as a last resort. Don't waste any more time here. Get everyone inside because, by the sound of those shots, we are soon going to be surrounded.'

9

Dwyer winced as a man splashed tequila on his wounded ear and wiped it none too gently with a bloodstained bandanna. The discomfort, he told himself, was nothing compared to what Robert E. Grant would suffer. Nobody would swindle Colonel Miguel Dwyer and live. He had paid good American dollars for five cases of carbine ammunition. The top case had contained rifle ammunition which the army had been giving free to buffalo shooters and the remaining cases had contained gravel. In the midst of a battle with Federal troops was not the time to discover that the fresh ammunition he had counted upon was all but useless. His revolutionaries had eagerly seized the new cartridges, but a couple of rounds had left them battered and in many cases gun-shy. It was a brave man who did not flinch when firing the full rifle round in a light carbine. Under such much-reduced and erratic fire, the shaken soldiers had recovered their confidence and forced Dwyer's men into an ignominious flight.

Now he had another problem. A minority of his riders still had a few rounds of carbine ammunition, but nowhere near enough for a sustained battle against trained infantry. His men possessed three Winchester repeaters but again, their ammunition supply was low.

Juan hurried over to where his leader was having his wounded ear treated. 'Things are not good, Colonel,' he reported. 'We cannot fight these men at long range. They have more rifle ammunition than we have.'

'Tell the men to work closer. There is enough brush on the hillsides to get into revolver range. Then we can rush them, as they only have single-shot rifles.'

The grizzled lieutenant shook his

105

head. 'That might not be a good idea. They have some revolvers,' he said doubtfully.

Dwyer waved a hand impatiently. 'They are not veteran fighters like our men. We need more fighting and less talking. I'll join you in a minute and we will plan an attack.'

'It is very dangerous, Colonel. That coach will already be missed and soldiers or lawmen will soon be looking for it. The gringos hold the water and our horses have much travelling to get us back over the border. We should cut our losses and go.'

'No,' Dwyer told him angrily. 'Who will follow me if I allow this man Grant to escape and leave the death of my cousin unavenged? We have lost good men. These people must pay. Our men expect no less.'

'Our men mainly expect to get back to Mexico with whole skins. If people think you would throw away their lives they will not follow you.'

Reluctantly Dwyer was forced to

admit the truth of Juan's argument. 'I suppose you are right. I will try one more attack here and if that fails, we will retreat.'

★ ★ ★

For the besieged there was a degree of relief. The travellers shared some of the soldiers' rations which, although very basic, were a great improvement on starvation.

The besiegers' rate of fire slackened considerably but the group at the well were careful not to take unnecessary risks. Careless movements between the ruins, the stake corral and the well still invited a bullet but the attackers were not wasting ammunition.

Jones had taken Wilmot's bandoleer and found that it contained only two rounds suitable for the carbine he carried. His own bandoleer yielded another three. The remaining cartridges were rifle rounds and these he placed to one side, to be used for only desperate, close-range work.

Chris found himself beside a soldier whom Quinn had left inside the adobe walls. The man indicated Jones and said quietly, 'I'm glad we have him on our side. He's hell on wheels with a gun.'

'Do you know him?'

'Only by sight,' the man admitted. 'I saw him kill a man in El Paso. The man he shot was supposed to be a mighty tough *pistolero* but that *hombre* there shot faster and straighter.'

'What were they fighting about?'

'I don't know,' the man admitted, 'but the law didn't seem all that interested in him. He had a couple of Mexicans with him and was driving a wagon. He went over the border into Mexico not long after the shooting. I don't reckon I ever heard his name but I'm sure that's the same man.'

A bullet came through the opening that once had held a door. It hit the wall just above Maggie's head and she shrieked in surprise as she was showered with adobe dust.

Amos grabbed her and none too gently pulled her away from the doorway. 'Did you get hit?' he demanded.

Maggie regained her composure and brushed the dust from her face and the shoulders of her blouse. 'I just got a fright. I'm not hurt.'

Chris was worried because the attackers would have been well around their position before a rifleman could angle a shot through the doorway. The sniper would be somewhere in the brush and could be as close as one hundred yards away.

He called to the soldiers in the corral. 'Did anyone see whcre that last shot came from?'

It was Ellen who answered his question. 'I saw a puff of smoke at the base of the hill. I'll show you.'

'Don't do that,' Chris said sharply. 'He could be waiting for someone to look around the corner of the doorway. Can you remember anything about the place where you saw it?'

The girl thought for a while. 'There's

a very tall, straight cactus just to the right of where I saw the smoke. It goes a fair way up before any branches come off it. It was somewhere near the bottom of that.'

The guard called to the soldiers in the corral. 'Can anyone see a tall, straight cactus on the flat across the road? We think there's a sniper somewhere to the left of it. He's firing through the doorway here.'

Quinn called back. 'That cactus is only about sixty yards away. He's mighty close.'

Another shot came from the brush behind the ruins. A soldier facing that way fired back before shouting, 'They're on this side too.'

The firing increased in intensity with puffs of smoke erupting from the brush disturbingly close to the besieged position. A couple of bullets fell short but others whined off stony ground, smacking against the adobe or burying themselves in the rotting wooden stakes of the corral.

'They're firing revolvers,' Jones told Chris. 'They could be getting ready to rush us. They know the soldiers have to reload after every shot.'

Chris saw the danger too. 'We can give some covering fire to the soldiers, but with only a door and a window to shoot through, we are likely to get in each other's way.'

Horace provided the answer to the problem. He indicated a couple of empty boxes that had held supplies. 'If we stand on those, we can shoot over the top of the wall.'

Amos appropriated one box and placed it firmly against the base of the ruined wall at one of its low points. 'I'm the tallest,' he said. 'So I reckon I can shoot over here easier than most.'

Horace took the other box and found a suitably low spot on the opposite wall.

Jones said that he would back up the soldier positioned at the window leaving Chris and Wilmot to guard the door. The latter was pale and glancing nervously about him, as though looking for an escape route or somewhere to hide. There were neither.

The besiegers' shots had slowed noticeably as they ensured that all their guns were loaded before making the final rush.

Suddenly a wild shout echoed around the narrow valley and pistol shots sounded on three sides.

'Here they come!' a soldier yelled.

10

Men sprang from the brush alarmingly close to the ruins and sprinted across the open ground. Occasionally one stopped to fire a shot but mostly they just ran, anxious to close the distance as the soldiers reloaded their single-shot rifles.

One man scarcely went three paces before a bullet cut him down, another staggered as though hit but then recovered and lurched forward again. Amos shot him from over the top of the wall.

Chris had no trouble selecting a target but one of the soldiers beat him to the shot and he saw the man smashed backwards by a powerful rifle bullet. Suddenly two men were converging on the open doorway. The first almost ran on to the muzzle of the guard's carbine and a squeeze of the trigger sent a .44 slug into him taking him out of the fight. A rattle of rapid shots from behind the guard sent the other attacker reeling away with one arm hanging uselessly. Good, he thought, Wilmot had at last decided to help.

Jones had taken over the window while the soldier with him reloaded his rifle, but the attack on that side seemed to have melted away.

Three Mexicans had reached the corral and were firing through the gaps between the stakes while Quinn and his men fired back and reloaded as quickly as they could.

Horace, who was shooting over the wall and had a better view of the corral, shouted urgently. 'Help the soldiers.'

Seeing no adversaries in front, Chris stepped out of the door and turned to his right. He could see the corral wreathed in gunsmoke and three attackers firing into it. At a few yards range, he raked them with rapid fire from his Winchester. One man crumpled forward while another was knocked flat on his back. The third turned to run but with the guard, Horace and a couple of soldiers shooting at him he was cut down after a couple of strides.

Somewhere in the brush a voice called loudly in Spanish and, as swiftly as they had arrived, the attackers were gone, leaving seven of their number sprawled on the ground. One man moved feebly and a soldier immediately fired another shot into him. The movement stopped.

'Cease firing,' Quinn bellowed. He turned to Amos. 'Are any of your folks hurt?'

The lanky driver looked around. He saw Wilmot edging out from behind Maggie. 'We have one nearly dead of fright, but that's all.'

Chris looked behind him and was surprised to see that it was Ellen standing there and not the man who was supposed to back him up.

The girl, despite her pale face and shaking hands, smiled apologetically and held up her empty revolver. 'I've run out of bullets.'

Angrily Chris looked about for Wilmot and found him standing sheepishly beside Maggie. The latter looked annoyed.

'Where the hell were you, Wilmot? How is it that you left a lady to do your share of the fighting?'

Though still pale, Larry answered in an aggrieved tone: 'Don't get too high-handed with me. Maggie was the only one without a gun and needed to be protected.' His courage might have deserted him but his wits had not.

The guard would have said more but there was a gentle touch on his arm. 'Don't worry,' Ellen said. 'We seem to have driven them off again so our luck is still holding.'

Two of the soldiers had been wounded. One had taken two bullets in his right arm and the other had been hit in the side. Both were stretched on the ground, their faces masks of shock and pain.

Quinn, conscious that another attack

could be imminent, reorganized his defenders after moving the wounded into the ruins, where they would have better protection.

Jones seemed to have more knowledge of bullet wounds than any of the others and, assisted by Ellen and Maggie, he took over the task of attending to the wounded.

With Amos and Wilmot keeping watch, Chris checked on the fallen Mexicans and collected their guns and ammunition. Aware that he could be a target for a rifleman, he worked swiftly collecting three revolvers and gun belts and passing two through the stakes to the soldiers. He told them: 'You might want to load these and keep them handy in case they attack again.'

'Do you think they will come again?' Private Ridley asked.

'I don't know. I wouldn't if I was them, but these characters have been mighty unpredictable.'

★　★　★

At the southern end of the valley Dwyer saw his men assembling. The defeated look on their faces told him that any further attacks would be futile. While his men might die for the ideals of their revolution, none would relish the idea of dying for the sake of their leader's reputation. But Miguel Dwyer was a single-minded man when he set himself a task. Robert E. Grant would yet be brought to account.

Quickly he called his men together and selected two whom he knew to be reliable men with a good command of the English language.

Morillo was barely twenty, short and wiry with strong Indian features but was both intelligent and skilled in guerrilla fighting. Correnza was older and slightly taller but he too had proved his worth in many skirmishes especially the more recent ones that had proved so costly.

'You ride with me,' the colonel told them. Then turning to his lieutenant he said, 'Juan, you must take the rest of the men back over the border. The Americanos will soon have troops after us and I want you to deceive them into thinking that our entire force has retreated. Lay false trails to delay them but leave enough traces for their scouts to follow. Take the spare horses because they must think they are following our whole band.'

'Sí, Colonel. But what will you be doing? Where will we rendezvous in Mexico?'

Dwyer replied: 'I will capture this Robert Grant person and meet you later at our camp in the Sierra Madres. Now go and leave a good trail at first for the cavalry to see. We will ride with you for a short distance and will split away at some place where the tracks won't show.'

Juan looked worried. 'But you don't know this Grant person.'

'We will follow these gringos. He will betray himself sooner or later and when he does, I will have him.'

'But people will see you,' Juan protested.

A smile flitted across Dwyer's face. 'It does not matter. There are plenty of gringo clothes left at that coach and probably some at the change station as well. Our clothes will make us look as though we have lived this side of the border for a long time and there are plenty of our people in New Mexico and Arizona. We will hide from the army right under their noses. Now we must go.'

* * *

Chris had been busy with his pocket-knife making new holes in the Mexican cartridge belt he had appropriated. The attached holster contained a Colt pocket revolver converted to take a .32 rim-fire cartridge.

Ellen had done all she could to help the wounded men and now was seated on a box in the ruins eating beans from a can. With a dirty face and dishevelled clothes she scarcely resembled the young lady who had boarded the coach on the previous day. There was sauce around her mouth and she had managed to spill some on her blouse but to the shotgun guard, she still looked as beautiful as ever.

'I have something for you,' he announced.

The girl stopped eating and looked up curiously.

'Seeing as how you backed me up so well today, I thought you might like a better gun. I made some extra holes in the belt so it should fit you. I wish it could be a bunch of flowers or something nice.' Chris's voice faltered as he suddenly wondered whether a dead man's gun was an appropriate gift for a lady. He continued lamely, 'It's a good gun, like the one you used today, except that it takes metallic cartridges — I thought it might be useful.'

A dazzling smile dispelled the guard's doubts. A small hand reached up and took the holstered weapon. 'That's very kind of you, Chris. I hope I will never have to use it but it will be a great souvenir. Thank you. As soon as I finish these beans, I'll get you to show me how to load and unload it. Have you eaten yet?'

'The soldiers are arranging some food for me now. Even that army grub will go down well.'

'Do you think those men will attack again?'

Chris looked around at the attackers still sprawled where they had fallen. Pausing a moment, he said, 'I'm not sure. Corporal Quinn reckons they need more men than he thinks they have. But there's something different about these characters. They know something about us that we don't.'

'They might know about me,' Ellen suggested. 'I'm carrying six hundred dollars in cash to make the final payment on our ranch mortgage. I wonder though how they would know about that.'

'I think it's more than a robbery.

Those Mexicans seemed more interested in catching up with someone
they called Robert E. Grant. That's a
fake name if ever I heard one. Either
they have been barking up the wrong
tree completely or one of our passengers has been in some sort of crooked
deal and double-crossed them somehow.'

'Horace and Larry are well-known
around the district and John Jones
seems a very decent type. The Mexicans
must be mistaken.'

'Being well-known at home doesn't
mean that they are known at all in
Mexico. These *hombres* are revolutionaries and can't check on every one who
does a deal with them. South of the
border they have to accept any name a
man uses if he is selling them
something they know is illegal.'

A shout from a soldier on watch
stopped any further conversation.

'There's dust rising behind that hill.
There's horses on the road causing
that. I think they could be coming
again.'

Ellen jumped to her feet and started buckling the gunbelt around her waist. 'I think you'd better show me how to load my new gun.'

11

They waited anxiously with all eyes fixed on the road where it passed over the hill. If it was the revolutionaries returning to the fight, they must surely have been reinforced, for a frontal attack straight down the road was guaranteed to be costly.

Horsemen appeared, a pair of them both in army blue. One by one the soldiers began to uncock their rifles. Then a wagon came over the crest.

'It's our transport,' a soldier said in a relieved tone. 'We're going home.'

A cavalry sergeant and an infantry lieutenant rode ahead of the canvas-topped wagon with its six-mule team. They urged their horses into a canter when they saw the scene before them. The battle casualties confirmed what the riders had expected but the presence of civilians among the soldiers took them by surprise.

The officer reined in his horse. 'Corporal Quinn. What has happened here?'

'There's been one hell of a fight, sir, and we have a couple of casualties. These other folks are from a coach attacked by Mexican rebels on the Holford road. They tracked them to here and we had quite a fight. We had two wounded but the Mexes lost a lot more and decided to pull out. They were here only a few minutes ago. You've only just missed them.'

'We know that,' the officer said as he dismounted. 'We saw them from a distance. Most of our cavalry escort is on their trail. We thought they might have come this way.'

The officer, Rodney Bell, was a handsome young man with fair hair and a neatly trimmed moustache. He instinctively straightened into a more military pose when he saw Ellen appear from behind the others.

Chris noted the gesture and felt a

126

twinge of jealousy. You are being stupid, he told himself. You hardly know the girl.

Amos introduced himself and asked, 'What made you think those *hombres* might be around here?'

'Our friends got too smart for their own good,' Bell told him. 'They were running us ragged with fake telegraph messages sending us away from where we should have been. One of our operators realized that there was an impostor on the line and somehow the engineers figured out where he would be. A cavalry patrol found our man just packing up his equipment. He tried to escape but was mortally wounded. He admitted that his name was Harvey Thomas and that he had been a signaller in the Confederate army but that was all he would tell us before he died. By sending us where he wanted us to go he gave a good indication of where he did not want us to be. Knowing that, it didn't take a genius to send patrols into this area.'

Jones had joined the conversation and still looked puzzled. At last he asked, 'With everyone using the same code, how could your man know there was a stranger hooked into the line?'

The officer explained. 'It appears that every operator has a different style of sending code. One of our men realized that he was getting messages from an operator who was not who he claimed to be.'

'Sounds like this Thomas character was not very smart,' Amos commented.

Bell disagreed. 'He was smart enough but conditions have changed. Signallers in wartime dealt with so many different operators in so many different places that they did not get time to recognize individual styles. It was only in peacetime, when operators stayed put and talked to the same people day after day that the touch of different individuals became easily recognized.'

'It sounds a bit too clever for me,' Horace observed. 'It's getting so respectable crooks won't be able to make a livin' soon.'

'Do you really think that's bad?' Wilmot asked incredulously.

'Don't worry, Larry. I'm sure smart crooks like you will always find a way to stay ahead of the law.'

'Who are you calling a crook?' Wilmot went red-faced with anger.

The tall driver intervened. 'Just settle down, you pair. I've just had enough fighting to last me a lifetime. When we get this mess fixed you can kill each other for all I care. But right now you are company responsibility, so I'm looking after your welfare — and if one of you jackasses steps out of line, I'll murder him myself.'

Jones chuckled. 'I think you are taking exactly the right approach, Amos.'

'What happens now?' Chris asked the lieutenant.

Bell thought a while. 'I suppose I will have to get the wounded and the civilians to Holford.'

'We won't all fit in the wagon, sir,' Quinn reminded him.

'I know that, Corporal. I'll leave your detail here to bury those dead men. I'll send a wagon back for you. Now we had better get the wagon loaded. The sooner we get the wounded to medical help, the better.'

Jones stood for a second staring down the road as if expecting Dwyer's men to reappear. 'It just dawned on me,' he told Horace. 'With that Thomas *hombre*, dead, we'll never know whether one of us was Robert E. Grant or it was just a case of mistaken identity.'

'Who cares?' the other replied with a shrug of his shoulders. 'It's all over now.'

$$\star \quad \star \quad \star$$

The three riders reined in their mounts among a clump of Joshua trees and looked down the mountain they had just ascended. Lower on the slopes and moving away from them, they could see the dust that the cavalry patrol had raised. Dwyer considered himself very lucky.

With his two companions he had scarcely left the main group when the wagon and a cavalry patrol came into view. Morino and Carrenza had wanted to flee but their leader told them to stay quietly under cover. A couple of hundred paces ahead, Juan and his men were only partly concealed on the mountainside. If the cavalry were halfway observant they would see them and give chase. And that was exactly what happened.

The watchers saw troopers pointing up the hillside, a brief flurry among the soldiers as someone gave orders and the riders in blue turned their mounts after Juan and his men.

'We stay here until there are no soldiers in sight,' the colonel said. 'They will have a long chase before they can run down Juan. He will lead them well away from us.'

'Juan's horses are very tired,' Morino said doubtfully.

Carrenza was more optimistic. 'The cavalry horses are carrying much more weight. Juan knows that and he will make sure that he uses the country in a way that will tire the soldiers' horses more than ours. He is as cunning as an Apache.'

'It was strange that so many soldiers came this way,' Dwyer told them. 'It was almost as if they knew where we would be.'

Morillo expressed a doubt that was beginning to form in Dwyer's mind. 'Do you think that Thomas might have betrayed us?'

Anger flashed across the colonel's face. 'He is as good as dead if he did.' Then he gathered up his reins and turned his mount toward the crest of the mountain. 'The soldiers are gone now. There's no time to waste. We must get to that coach before anyone else comes along.'

Two hours later the trio halted at what was now a ghastly scene. The bloated carcasses of the dead horses were rotting in the sun and a cloud of buzzards reluctantly rose as the men urged their nervously snorting mounts closer. The bullet-scarred coach stood abandoned like a wrecked vessel stuck on a reef.

Morillo made a disgusted grimace and waved a hand in front of his face. 'Breathe through your mouth, *amigo*,' he said to Carrenza. 'It probably tastes better than it smells.'

Dwyer seemed impervious to the unpleasantness of the scene and noted with satisfaction that the baggage in the boot of the coach had not been disturbed. He had forbidden any looting in the rush to capture Grant. Now his decision had paid off, although it had been the cause of much discontent at the time.

The three worked quickly unloading the bags and carrying them to a place upwind from the dead horses. Under a shady tree they broke open the suitcases.

'Now,' Dwyer announced. 'Let us see

if we can find clothes to fit and we will start looking like gringos. The army will be looking for *bandidos* but we will look like respectable citizens.'

It did not take long for the three to find clean clothes that fitted well enough to satisfy a cursory glance. Most important, the new attire would change their obvious Mexican appearance. Each man selected a clean shirt and trousers, Morillo found a new vest that fitted him and Dwyer appropriated a coat that had belonged to Jones.

Carrenza was about to begin changing but his leader stopped him. 'Find razors and boot polish if there is any. Then we will go to the stage station, clean ourselves up and change.'

'Colonel,' Morillo ventured nervously. 'Do we really need to waste time shaving and cleaning boots?'

'We do. The army will be looking for unshaven, dirty fugitives. They will not look twice at cleanly dressed men. We are about to become respectable.'

'There is one problem,' Morillo

reminded him. 'Our sombreros will look out of place with these gringo clothes.'

'I thought of that. Those stage company men at the change station both had hats. We will collect those when we go there. If you have a sombrero it will not matter. We cannot disguise your Indian features. Three of our people might attract attention but one in the company of two gringos will not. Now get your new clothes and we will go to the change station. We can't leave our old clothes here because someone might realize that we have changed. Later we will dump them.'

'But where are we going?' Carrenza asked.

'We go back and pick up the tracks of that wagon. This Grant man will be in it. Where it goes, we go.'

12

Holford was a far from thriving metropolis but it looked heavenly to those who had endured a long bumpy ride in an army wagon. Despite all efforts to make them comfortable, the wounded men had suffered badly, so all agreed that they should be unloaded first at the small infirmary run by the two local doctors.

The travellers disembarked at the town's largest hotel where Amos arranged meals for them before hurrying off to the stage company's office. The service had been suspended because of the emergency but Barney Rule, the Holford manager, had kept open the office hoping to hear some news of the missing coach. His homely face with its luxuriant sidewhiskers, broke into a relieved smile when Amos walked in the door. A flurry of questions followed as each sought to find out the current situation.

Amos was mostly concerned with the well-being of the passengers but Rule was more worried about the condition of the coach. 'Our services have been suspended,' he said. 'Head Office won't like this. We have been losing money over the last couple of days.'

'We'll lose a hell of a lot more if one of those passengers gets a sharp lawyer, Barney. Let's get some telegraph messages to the company so I can tell my passengers what's going on. They've been mighty patient up till now but I reckon there's a couple among them who might sue for damages if they have too much time to think.'

'Get them fed and arrange hotel rooms for any not finishing their journey here in Holford,' the agent said. 'You and your guard can bunk down here at the depot.'

The travellers had finished eating when Amos returned to the hotel. He had spent the last hour with Barney harassing the telegraph operator to get quick answers from the company management to the many problems the recent happenings had thrown up.

'The Rutherford Stage Company is suspending operations,' the driver announced, 'but the company will pick up the hotel bills for any passengers who are travelling further and who are delayed until another coach is available.'

'What about our lost luggage?' Maggie demanded.

'That's right,' Wilmot said in support. 'I had a lot of expensive clothes and other valuable personal items in my bag.' Already he was seeing a means of making a profit out of the misadventure.

Horace chuckled. 'They won't get much out of my bag, maybe a clean shirt and some well-worn socks and my second-best pair of pants.'

The driver continued: 'In the morning, me and Chris and Sheriff Brunskill are riding out to the coach to see what can be retrieved. We are taking a team with us, and whatever can be salvaged we will bring back here. We will collect all the baggage so the owners can sort it out.'

'What if things are damaged or missing?' Wilmot demanded.

'That's a job for the company lawyers. You might have to fight that out with them.'

Maggie did not relish that idea but was suddenly very tired and lost any inclination to argue. In a resigned manner she said: 'I'm not sure there'll be anything of value left in my baggage after Mexican bandits have been through it. Right now though I'm aching all over and am only interested in a night's rest.'

Chris had carefully manoeuvred himself so that he was seated beside Ellen. 'What are your plans now?' he asked.

'I can go ahead and attend to my business here tomorrow, although I'll cause a fright going into the bank looking like this. When the stages start running again, I'll go back to Muddy Creek, but until then I am stuck here. What about you?'

'A lot will depend on what we find tomorrow, but my home base is at Muddy Creek so I might see you there. Do you live in town?'

'No, my folks have a cattle ranch a few miles out on Mustang Creek. Pa never had much education so I do a lot of the ranch business. I'm in Holford to settle our mortgage. By this time tomorrow our ranch will be free of debt.'

'That would be a big relief to your folks.'

'That's right and it's thanks to you and Amos that I still have the means to settle the mortgage.'

Chris felt some satisfaction from that but fatigue was weighing heavily upon him and he could think of no more relevant conversation. With a mumbled excuse he took his leave of the group. The next day was sure to be busy and any sleep he could grab before then suddenly seemed very precious.

* * *

They started next morning before sunrise. Chris and Amos rode astride a couple of ride-and-drive horses and led a spare horse each. These would comprise the four-horse team that would take the coach and whatever could be salvaged back to Holford.

Sheriff Brunskill, a heavily built, short man with a lined face reminiscent of a worried bloodhound rode with them. He was getting close to retirement and did not appreciate any undue excitement in his jurisdiction.

'Damnit, Amos,' he complained, 'I'm getting too old for all this riding about. I wish you'd arranged for them road agents to jump you in some other sheriff's territory.'

The tall driver laughed. 'Next time I will, Fred. I didn't have a lot of say about where this little ruckus happened.'

'Have you heard whether the army caught up with our Mexican friends?' Chris asked.

The sheriff shook his head. 'Nothing has come over the telegraph but then nobody tells me anything. Those rebels could have captured Washington and I would be the last to know.'

They saw the buzzards circling long before they reached the change station and knew there was no chance that the two men who worked there would be alive. Some distance further away more buzzards circled in the cloudless blue sky. These marked the location of the coach and its dead team.

Chris pointed in that direction. 'There are probably a few dead revolutionaries near the coach if their *compadres* didn't take the time to plant them.'

'I reckon that General Dwyer, or whatever he calls himself, will think twice before he pokes his nose over the border again,' Brunskill told them.

Passing through a gap between two

hills, the riders found themselves looking south with a saw-toothed range of hills on their right. Amos waved vaguely in their direction. 'We came over them hills the night before last,' he told the sheriff. 'If you look ahead at that big patch of cottonwoods you can just make out the roof and part of the change station corrals.'

The stench of death greeted them as they approached the silent buildings and the horses snorted nervously. The mangled remains of the station's two-man staff lay sprawled a few paces from the open door of the main building.

'Looks like someone took them both by surprise,' Brunskill observed. 'There are no ejected shells or signs of any gunfight. They're close together and must have died at much the same time. If they were carrying guns, their killers must have taken them.'

Amos swore under his breath. He had known both men. Their murders were bad enough but leaving their bodies to scavengers rankled even more.

Chris and the sheriff did not know either man so the driver would be forced to identify the victims. The guard held the horses while the other pair began their gruesome task. Buzzards, coyotes and foxes had not made identification easy but Amos recognized items of clothing that the men had worn and was able to provide names for the sheriff to note in his book.

'We'd better go inside the station now and see what other nasty surprises we find.' Brunskill closed the cover of his book and walked to the open door. The driver followed him.

Chris had intended putting the horses in the corral and joining the others inside when he noticed something odd about some nearby horse tracks. Being made in soft dust they did not retain sharp edges for long and he noticed that some looked much more recent. There were boot tracks there too.

When Brunskill emerged, he called him over and indicated the tracks. 'I think that someone has been here fairly recently.'

'There's been a whole heap of them here,' the sheriff told him. 'They took everything they thought might be useful. You don't need to be an Injun tracker to see that. They're long gone from here now.'

Chris was still inclined to argue. 'Some of these tracks don't look as old as the others. I reckon a few could have been made last night.'

'Well, I ain't worrying if they were. Those *bandidos* were headed south with the army on their heels. They wouldn't come back this way. Maybe a couple of saddle tramps came through but the pickings would be mighty lean. There's nothing of any real value left inside. Amos is doing a final check for company property and such and then we'll have to plant these men. Put the horses in the corral and see if you can find some shovels in the barn.'

The funeral was a hasty affair. While the sheriff wrapped the bodies in old tarpaulins he found in the barn, the stage company men were digging the graves. The ground was hard and as the sun climbed higher the heat intensified. The unaccustomed work with crowbars and shovels raised blisters on the sweating gravediggers' hands but at last the holes were deep enough.

Amos stood panting from the exertion while Chris helped carry the dead men to their temporary resting place. The heavy physical activity of the last couple of days was taking its toll on both men but the driver was really feeling his advancing years.

When both corpses were lowered into the graves, Brunskill grabbed a shovel. He volunteered to fill in the holes while the others retrieved the coach.

'Ain't you gonna read over them or something?' Amos asked. These were men he had known and he felt that they deserved better than a hasty interment.

The sheriff shook his head. 'I didn't

bring no Bible and I don't think it matters all that much. Wherever this pair are going, they'd be there by now. If relatives should want them dug up and planted somewhere else, I reckon they can organize a preacher for them then. Now, get going and get back here as soon as you can. It's a long ride back to Holford.'

13

The scene when they reached the abandoned coach was one of desolation. Apart from the dead horses, the luggage had been taken from the boot and rifled. Articles of clothing, both male and female, were scattered about and again the stench of death hung over the scene.

They dismounted and Amos examined the coach. The vehicle had several bullet holes in it but structurally it was sound. One wheel-spoke had been broken by a bullet but the driver was confident that the wheel would hold up because the coach would only be lightly loaded.

With much effort and no small amount of bad language they managed to get the harness off the dead animals and transfer it to the horses they had brought with them. Before hooking the team to the coach Amos held them while Chris collected the scattered clothing and stuffed it back into suitcases. He kept the ladies' attire in a couple of bags and the men's in the remainder so that their owners could sort out who owned what when they brought it to Holford. When all was gathered together they hooked the team's traces to the coach and Amos did his customary check on the buckles. Chris held the leaders' heads until the driver was in his seat and had gathered up his reins. Then he took his place on the box beside Amos. Both men were relieved when the team stepped out on command and the coach started rolling again. They knew that the corpses of some of their late attackers were nearby but both agreed that they were not the responsibility of the Rutherford Stage Company.

Brunskill had filled in the graves by the time they arrived back at the station. He was glad to see the coach arrive.

'I should be used to things like this now,' he told the others, 'but this was kind of creepy. I was wondering about those tracks you saw, Chris, and started imagining what would happen if those killers came back and caught me on my lonesome.'

Amos suggested: 'Tie your horse on behind and ride back with us. This team's fresh and we should make good time.'

'I'll take you up on that offer,' Brunskill said. 'I'm getting too old to enjoy long rides.'

★ ★ ★

Larry Wilmot was enjoying himself. Suddenly he was a celebrity and the number of bandits he claimed to have killed or put to flight increased with every free drink that was thrust upon him. Horace had also solicited a few free drinks but said little. As though amused by Wilmot's claims, he was smiling as he leaned against the bar

150

and sipped his whiskey. He noticed the earnest young reporter from the *Holford Clarion* scribbling frantically in his notebook and knew that soon a lurid version of their experiences would be spread throughout the south-west. John Jones had the right idea, Horace thought. He was keeping a low profile and was avoiding the attention that Wilmot was enjoying.

Another spectator stood silently at the back of the crowd. A tall dark man with a clean new bandage around his head and extending over his damaged right ear. Dwyer had visited both the town doctor and a barber and now bore little resemblance to a hunted man. He saw the onlooker he wanted, a cowhand by the look of him, one who was likely to be less suspicious of his own kind. Casually he asked, 'What's all the fuss about?'

The cowhand glanced at him and replied, 'That loud-mouthed *hombre* there is tellin' us how he fought off a whole bunch of Mexican bandits.' The man paused and looked at Dwyer. 'You look like you've been doin' some fightin' yourself.'

'A half-broke bronc bogged his head with me when I was riding under a low tree. A sharp branch damn near ripped off my ear.'

The cowboy nodded sympathetically. 'I've seen that happen a time or two but fortunately it ain't happened to me yet.'

Dwyer brought him back to the present. 'Did that *hombre* fight off those outlaws all on his own?'

'Hell, no. That untidy feller leanin' on the bar was with him. He's from Muddy Creek. His name's Horace Weldon. We all know him around here. He's quite a character but most folks reckon he ain't too bad. There was another passenger too, a feller named John Jones, but he don't seem to like publicity. He kept pretty much to himself, had one drink and vamoosed as though he wanted to keep away from the other pair. I heard though that the coach crew and the army helped that Wilmot feller defeat those Mexican hordes.'

'Do you know why Mexican revolutionaries would be on this side of the border?'

'Not really,' the cowboy admitted, 'but it was probably money. I heard one of the lady passengers had a whole heap of cash on her. The bandits missed that.'

Until that moment Dwyer had thought that the three men were the only suspects but now the field had widened. The woman could be in cahoots with Robert E. Grant and might even have been transferring his ill-gotten gains to a safer place. That prospect seemed unlikely but it had to be considered. Then there was the matter of his cousin's death. 'Did that loud-mouthed character kill all those Mexicans by himself?'

'No, but he would like us to think so. I heard that the shotgun guard, a feller named Unwin, accounted for at least three bandits. Some say he might have shot others too, but at this stage I don't think anyone knows the full story.'

The cowboy knew no more so Dwyer casually mingled with some of the other drinkers, listening for snippets of information. Sticking close to the reporter and Wilmot, he heard the latter say that the passengers were all staying at the hotel until the coaches started running again.

Satisfied with what he had learned the revolutionary quietly finished his drink and left the saloon. His next stop would be the hotel.

★ ★ ★

The four-horse team was making easy work of the lightly loaded coach and the three men on the box were thinking only of getting back to Holford. They still had a long journey ahead when Chris suddenly pointed to the left side of the road which was partly screened by a wall of berry bushes. 'I can see

154

something ahead behind the bushes on this side. Just take it slowly, Amos.'

'Is it trouble?' the driver asked suspiciously.

'No. It's something shiny. It shouldn't be out here whatever it is. Stop when we get past that wall of bushes and I'll have a look.'

'Why waste time?' Amos growled. 'It's probably only a fish can that someone has thrown away.'

'This ain't the sort of place where folks stop to eat canned fish,' Brunskill said. 'Better pull up for a minute, Amos.'

Reluctantly the driver halted the team and his expression was far from happy when the other two climbed down.

When they found a gap in the tangle of vines and forced their way through, they discovered a couple of Mexican sombreros and three ragged pairs of trousers. Nearby were three torn shirts, one of them bloodstained.

One sombrero was of good quality

with silver braid around the brim and a silver-decorated band. Chris picked it up and pointed to the band. 'That's what I saw shining.' He looked closer and saw a hole in the brim and what looked like a bloodstain. Something stirred in his memory. 'I think I saw this hat before. The leader of those Mexicans was wearing it. I took a shot at him but thought I missed. You can see the bullet hole and if that's a bloodstain, I must have nicked him on the side of the head.'

Brunskill looked around. 'I wonder if those *hombres* might have changed into some clothes they took from the baggage on the coach and didn't want anyone to know. Anyone passing on the trail would not be able to see over these bushes. It was only because we were up high on the coach that we were able to see them. I don't blame them though for wanting to change out of those rags they left behind.'

Chris looked about him but saw nothing else before replying, 'What worries me is what they changed into. I think these characters will be a lot harder to spot now. And there's another thing — they're going the wrong way for men supposed to be heading for the border.'

Brunskill shrugged his shoulders. 'I've had plenty of practice at the man-hunting game, sonny, and men on the run often head in the wrong direction just to lay a false trail. They might head to the north but sooner or later they'll swing back to the south. It's possible that they did the old Injun trick of splitting up so they can make their run to the border in small groups.'

'What if these men are not heading for the border?' Chris was not convinced by the sheriff's argument. 'As I recall, they were mighty keen to catch up with a certain Robert E. Grant who was supposed to be on the coach. If they thought he was in Holford, they might still come after him. They seemed to want him pretty bad.'

'But there was no one by that name among the passengers.'

'No one who would admit to it but at least two of our male passengers were not the most upstanding citizens and one is almost certainly travelling under a false name.'

'If you're thinking of that Jones *hombre*, I'm two jumps ahead of you. I've been through all my wanted dodgers and he doesn't fit the description of any wanted man that I know about,' Brunskill said. 'It's likely that these Mexes got the wrong coach. Men hiding out in the brush don't always get the most recent information.'

Chris picked up the two sombreros. 'I'll take these along just in case we meet their owners in our travels. Now we'd better hurry back to Amos. He don't believe in waiting around with a coach and we are still a long way from Holford.'

The guard was right. Amos was glowering as he held the impatient team. 'Hurry up and get aboard you two. I don't want to be getting back to town in the dark.' He glanced at the two hats the guard was carrying. 'Collecting old hats now, are you?'

'This fancy one is not so old and I'm a bit puzzled as to why its owner left it behind. I'm also worried about where that man is now.'

'He's the least of our worries. Now, get up here on the box and stop wasting time. Chances are the company's trying to find us in Holford.'

The sheriff and the guard did as they were ordered but even then Amos set the team in motion before they had barely settled into their seats. At a steady trot, he guided the four horses through the lengthening shadows.

Though the older men appeared unconcerned, Chris felt a sense of unease that gradually increased as they neared Holford. He told himself that he was suffering from an over-active imagination but the discovery of the hats had started him wondering whether some threat still existed. It seemed most unlikely but he suspected that men like Dwyer survived for so long only by doing the unexpected.

14

Jones leaned against a veranda post outside the hotel and watched darkness fall as he smoked a cigar. One by one the lamps in the town buildings were lit and soon pools of yellow light seemed to be offering resistance to what promised to be a dark and moonless night. The saloon was too crowded and people were asking too many questions in there.

A few people passed but Jones took little notice. After the drama of the last couple of days the tension was going and he was beginning to relax again. Idly he watched two men approaching along the boardwalk. They did not appear to be together and one was several paces ahead of the other. As he passed by a lighted window a white bandage showed under the rearmost man's hat. Just someone in town having an injury treated, he told himself.

Dwyer had planned well. A few discreet enquiries at the hotel had established his target's identity and Jones had played into his hands by standing alone in the poorly lit street.

The first man had passed Jones but, to his surprise, the one with the bandage stopped and spoke to him.

'John Jones?'

'That's right. What can I do for you?'

'Come with me,' Dwyer said quietly. 'There is something I must ask you.'

'What do you want?' There was suspicion now in Jones's voice. It was tinged too with anger because he objected to being ordered about. But the hard muzzle of a gun against his spine told him that the first man had turned back and now had him covered.

'Follow me down that alley.' Dwyer pointed to the space between the hotel and the next building. 'I want to ask you some questions about a certain Robert E. Grant. Don't do anything stupid.'

Jones knew then that he had been captured by the revolutionaries and that, no matter what answers he gave, he would be unlikely to escape from his predicament alive. Fighting down feelings of panic, he mentally assessed his chances. The odds were stacked against him but he knew that the longer he delayed an escape bid, the less likely it was to succeed. He had to take the risk before his captors had him completely in their power.

The man behind him with the gun was not experienced in taking prisoners and was standing too close. Jones had heard law enforcement officers discussing the danger of pressing a gun against a prisoner's back. The chance was there and he knew that he had to take it. A slim chance was better than none at all.

The gun prodded again. Reluctantly Jones took a step and Dwyer, seeing his compliance, turned to lead the way into the alley. The gun muzzle was still pressed hard into the captive's back.

Summoning up all his nerve, Jones took a chance.

He pivoted on his right heel and at the same time his right elbow knocked the gun aside. Continuing the circular movement, he smashed his left fist into the gunman's face. The punch landed solidly and the man reeled away. By this time Jones was going for his own gun as he wheeled again to face Dwyer. It was clear of the holster and he was cocking the hammer but he had not counted on the speed of the other's reaction. Dwyer drew and fired as he rapidly faced about. The bullet hit Jones and staggered him but did not knock him off his feet. Desperately he righted himself in an attempt to return the fire but his movements were fatally slow.

Dwyer's next shot slammed the wounded man to the ground. Almost as a reflex action Jones fired back, but his bullet flew wide of the mark. Carrenza finally went into action, triggering two quick shots into the fallen man who shuddered under the impact of the bullets before collapsing limply in death.

Dwyer had an emergency plan for such a situation and ordered, 'Get out quick. Go straight down the alley. Morillo will take over now.'

By the time curious townspeople sought the source of the shooting the killers had slipped away into the darkness.

Then a dark figure unhitched a horse from the rail in front of the saloon and vaulted into the saddle. He fired across the faces of the other horses fastened to the rail. The muzzle flash caused several to pull back and break their bridles. Herd instinct and panic took over as the gunman spurred his mount out of town with the loose horses following.

'There he goes!' someone shouted.

A half-drunk cowhand started shooting in the wake of the fleeing rider but his companions restrained him in case he shot their horses which were partly shielding the fugitive.

None of the confused onlookers

realized what they were really seeing. Working to the prearranged plan in case of shooting, Morillo had noted the arrival of cowhands from nearby ranches. Their horses when set loose would gallop back to their home ranges and confuse anyone who might try to follow. When barely clear of town, the Mexican slipped the bridle from the horse he was riding, vaulted from its back and hit the ground running. He tripped on a piece of rough ground but had already broken his fall and rolled harmlessly along the soft earth for a short distance. A second later he was on his feet and brushing the dust from himself as he crept back towards the town lights.

By this time someone had found the slain man and confusion was reigning. Some were trying to organize a posse to pursue the 'murdering horse-thief' while others advocated awaiting Brunskill's arrival before deciding upon a course of action.

The coach arrived in the middle of

all the chaos. It halted briefly to allow Brunskill to alight and unhitch his horse. A crowd of men surrounded the sheriff, each shouting to make himself heard above the others.

Chris and Amos listened from their seats as men recounted the recent events. Seeing Horace in the crowd, Chris called to him. 'What's happening, Horace?'

'Someone let daylight through John Jones. He's stone dead.'

Amos was shocked. 'Who killed him?'

Horace moved closer to the coach so he did not have to shout so much. 'No one knows. The killer stole a horse and bolted out of town. It only happened a few minutes ago. Did you get any of our belongings?'

'There's some here. We'll take the coach down to the company office,' Amos told him. 'You can come down and sort out what's yours tomorrow. If you see him you could tell Larry Wilmot too.'

They continued to the barn behind

the company office. The regular staff had finished for the day but Amos was familiar with the barn and set about unhitching horses, hanging the harness on hooks and placing each animal in a stall with a good supply of feed.

Chris busied himself collecting the passengers' baggage and carrying it into the company office. He noted that the men's bags had been broken open and their contents scattered but the obviously feminine ones seemed relatively undisturbed. The locks had been broken but the clothes inside had been ignored. He told himself that the bandits had had no intention of taking pretty dresses back to their lady friends. They had more serious matters on their minds.

When their work was done the coach crew sought the nearest restaurant for a quick meal. The food was not particularly appetizing but they felt better after it.

Amos pushed back his chair and stood up. 'Now I reckon I'll have a drink or two before I turn in. Are you coming?'

'I sure am. I need something to wash away the taste of that hash we just had.'

The saloon, when they reached it, was not busy for it had been a working day. The shooting had lured a few drinkers away and those from the more distant ranches had already gone home. Consequently it was not hard to find Brunskill as he leaned on the bar talking to the bartender. His face lit up when he saw Chris. 'Just the man I wanted to see,' he announced. 'I was wondering if you would like to join my posse in the morning. I'm going out to try and find the man who shot that Jones feller. I can get a horse for you.'

'He can't,' Amos answered before Chris could reply. As senior company man he felt entitled to make decisions that affected his coach. 'We might have to start back for Muddy Creek tomorrow. The stage from the north arrives tomorrow with a strong-box to go back through to El Paso. We've been told to wait for a telegram with instructions. If the company thinks it's safe, we could be on the way home tomorrow.'

'Too bad,' the sheriff said and tossed down the last of his drink. 'I'll be leaving early so probably won't see you. At least you should have a safer trip now the army has chased those Mexicans away.'

Chris at last expressed the doubt that had been niggling at him since he heard of the Jones shooting. 'You don't suppose that Jones was this Grant character that Colonel Dwyer was after? The name John Jones sounds too plain to be real.'

Brunskill laughed. 'According to some papers I found on him, the late Mr Jones was really Wolfgang Guggenburger. If I had a moniker like that I wouldn't use it either. It might have sounded fine in Germany where his folks came from but it's a hell of a name to saddle an American kid with.'

Amos looked doubtful. 'That doesn't

clear him from being this Grant character. Seems to me that he's had a bit of practice using false names.'

'If that's the case, Dwyer got what he was after so the rest of you can relax.'

'What about the story Chris heard about Grant being a gunfighter?'

Brunskill shrugged his shoulders. 'Who knows? It might have been a case of mistaken identity, or it could have been true. If he was, it gives me a motive for his murder but it's nothing you need to worry about.'

'I sure hope you're right,' Chris said.

15

Wilmot was a little unsteady on his feet when he left the saloon where he had been holding court. The walk to the hotel was not a long one but he did not get there.

A calloused hand clamped over his mouth as he passed the entrance of a dark alley and the cold barrel of a gun was thrust against his head. Drunk though he was, he recognized the menace in the voice that told him to be silent. Almost paralysed with fear, he made no sound as his captor dragged him deeper into the blackness of the alley.

Two men and three saddled horses were waiting at the back of the buildings.

'If you make one sound,' Dwyer said softly, 'you will die.'

Wilmot did make one sound, a little

whimper of sheer terror but apparently that was permissible, because he was not killed.

His captors gagged him, tied his hands behind his back and hoisted him on to a horse. Another rope that went around his waist and the saddle horn was intended to keep him in the saddle but the colonel's instruction to his men was an added incentive to remain mounted.

'If he falls off, kill him. If he is still alive when you reach that place we found, one stays to guard him and the other brings back the horses. I'll be in my hotel room. Now get going and don't waste time. We have one more to take and one to kill.'

Ellen was not sleeping well. The bed was lumpy and uncomfortable and the sounds of guests coming and going and the opening and closing of doors were in stark contrast to the silent nights on the family ranch. She was not sure of the time when she heard the thumping of boot heels and the jingle of spurs outside in the corridor. Nervously she reached for the gun she had placed on a chair beside the bed but to her relief the footsteps continued. She heard them halt at the end of the hall somewhere near the room in which Horace was lodged at stage company expense. Probably a couple of drinking mates calling on Horace, she thought.

While still trying to get back to sleep she heard a knock on Horace's door, a murmur of voices and a rattle as the door opened. More sounds followed, low voices, a few bumping noises, the sound of the door closing again and footsteps retreating down the hall. As she sought to get to sleep she had the impression that Horace had not welcomed his drinking partners and had sent them on their way. She thought she heard horses in the yard below and imagined that someone would have a long ride home. Then she lapsed into sleep.

Chris was awake early in the morning. Amos had seen to that. He wanted his former passengers to come to the stage depot and sort out the belongings that the revolutionaries had mixed up and left with the stranded coach. The driver had an organized mind, and the sooner things returned to normal the happier he would be. Amos was also feeling the after-effects of his recent exertions. Bones and muscles were aching, he moved slowly and painfully and was not in the best of moods.

Glad of the opportunity to see more of Ellen, Chris volunteered to go to the hotel and advise the passengers that their baggage was ready to be claimed and collected.

Brunskill and four heavily armed men rode past just as the guard left the stage office. The sheriff seemed deep in thought and appeared not to notice Chris as he guided his tall black horse along the almost empty main street. The other posse members were talking among themselves as though enjoying the break to their normal routines.

Mentally Chris wished them success in their hunt. He had liked Jones and was still puzzled as to the motive behind his death.

He found Ellen and Maggie just leaving the dining room after breakfast. 'I was just coming to see you ladies. Amos and I brought the baggage in from the coach last night. It's down at the stage company office but it's kind of mixed up. You will need to go down there and sort out who owns what. Have you seen Horace and Larry Wilmot?'

'They weren't at breakfast,' Ellen said. 'I think that Horace got in very early this morning. It sounded like some cowhands were delivering him to his room. Most likely he's still sleeping. I don't know about Larry though.'

'I'll give them a call,' Chris said. 'I'll see you ladies later at the company office.'

He knew the room numbers, so he ascended the stairs and walked down the long hall to Horace's room. To his surprise the door was slightly ajar. When he knocked, it swung inwards. Even without entering, Chris could see that something was wrong.

The bed was dishevelled and a six-shooter was lying in the middle of the floor. Horace's gunbelt was near the bed but the holster was empty. One boot was beside the bed and the other was across the other side of the room. Horace's battered hat was still hanging on the back of a chair where he had probably hung it before retiring. It was quite in character for a man like Horace, when drunk, to remove boots, hat and gunbelt before collapsing on the bed. But he was unlikely to leave his room without his boots and hat and certainly would not leave his gun lying in the middle of the floor.

With a mounting sense of alarm, Chris went next door to Wilmot's room. The door was locked but no sleepy voice answered when he pounded on the door. He hurried back downstairs to the desk clerk and explained the situation. The middle-aged clerk did not hesitate but took a duplicate key to the room and led the way back up the stairs. As he went, he advised Chris that the desk had not been manned during the night as the only guests were the coach passengers. The man explained that with the stage company picking up the costs there was no danger that the tenants would disappear without paying their bills. When he opened the door, they could see that Wilmot had not used his bed.

Chris knew that something was seriously wrong. Wilmot liked his comfort too much to be sleeping off a skinful of whiskey in some stable somewhere. And, rough though he was, Horace would not be walking around town without his hat, boots, or gun. 'Lock those rooms,' he told the clerk. 'Sheriff Brunskill might want to see in them later. I reckon Horace Weldon's met with foul play. I have to go back to the stage company office. If you find out anything I'd appreciate you sending word to me there.'

He ran back to the office where Ellen and Maggie had both checked and repacked their much battered suitcases.

'What's the hurry?' Amos demanded.

Still panting for breath. Chris replied, 'Horace and Wilmot — they're both gone — I think someone's taken them.'

The driver snorted in disbelief. 'Who would want to take that pair? There's folks would pay them to stay away.'

'What about that Mexican with the Irish name — Dwyer or whatever it was? He was mighty keen to meet some of our passengers.'

'He's running for his life with the army after him.'

'Maybe not. I've seen Indian war parties split up and send decoys everywhere. Dwyer could easily do the same. What if he hasn't given up the hunt for Robert E. Grant? This could be what his whole raid was about.'

Amos shook his head like an old angry bull. 'I don't give two hoots in hell what that crazy galoot is about, and as far as I'm concerned he's welcome to that pair of no-goods. It's none of our business what sorts of shady deals those two have been making.'

'I reckon it is our business, Amos. The Rutherford Stage Company is taking care of any passengers delayed here until the stages start running again. Legally we are responsible for them and this trip has cost the line a pile of dough already. If something happens to them and their relatives decide to sue us, this company won't have enough money to pay the damages. We'll both be out of a job.'

'Ain't a damn thing we can do,' the driver said stubbornly. 'Leave it all to Brunskill if they ain't showed up by the time he's back.'

'The sheriff might not be back for days. I'm going to see what I can find out before the trail gets too cold. I won't sit around waiting to see what someone in our head office thinks. I'm going to find out what happened to them if I can.'

'You might need to find a new job while you're at it,' Amos reminded him. 'The company would want you to wait for the sheriff.'

Chris turned and walked to the door of the office. 'To hell with the company. They can fire me as of now if they like. I think Horace and Wilmot are in real danger. But until I get word that I am fired, I'm borrowing a horse and saddle to take a look around.'

'Don't do anything rash, Chris. Those two are not the most reliable of characters and they'll probably turn up later with some far-fetched story about what happened to them. You don't even know Dwyer is around here.'

'He's here, or his men are here. That's why we found those hats. They might not look too much like Mexicans any more but I'll bet they've been here. I think they killed Jones and might already have killed Horace and Wilmot.'

Ellen took a hand in the conversation then. 'I might have heard Horace being taken from his room last night. I heard men going down the hall and there were horses behind the hotel under my window later. But I'm not sure what time it was.'

'Thanks, Miss Ellen,' Chris said. 'I'll go over there and have a look in case I can learn something from the tracks. I'd better go before someone walks all over them.'

'You're crazy,' Amos called after the guard as he left.

16

The tracks behind the hotel were those of three horses and, to Chris's relief, they led not to one of the well-used roads but to a brush-covered ridge west of the town. Someone seemed to be keen to avoid chance encounters on the regular roads. The tracks showed the horses travelling in single file so that the hoof marks were mixed up, but one animal left a distinctive trail. It had a dishing action and its near forefoot was placed slightly to the side of where a horse with a straight action would tread. Consequently the print showed clearly beside the other churned-up tracks. Because they had been travelling in the dark, the riders had left a trail of small broken branches that they could not avoid as they pushed through the brush in the night. Tracking would not be difficult.

Chris collected his Winchester and hurried to the company stables where Alf Correy was feeding the horses. The young stable hand could see that something urgent was afoot. 'Howdy, Chris. You look like a man in a hurry.'

'I need the loan of a good riding-horse, Alf. Do you have something that is not a hairy-heeled coacher?'

The groom indicated a red roan mare in a stall at the far end of the barn. 'You can take that roan mare. One of the company's agents bought her at a bargain price somewhere but she's too light for coach work. We keep her here strictly for riding purposes. The exercise will do her good. The saddles and bridles are over there on the other wall. Help yourself.'

Chris saddled the mare and was about to mount when Amos appeared, limping painfully with a disapproving frown on his face. 'You should be leaving this to Brunskill. I'm not sure that the company would approve of you going off on your own.'

The guard stepped into the stirrup and swung aboard the roan. 'Too bad if they don't. I might be barking up the wrong tree but I have to be sure because if I'm right things are looking mighty bad for Wilmot and Horace.'

The guard's argument seemingly convinced the older man. He paused a while, then said, 'Maybe I should be going with you, but after all the exertions of the last couple of days I can barely walk, let alone ride. I don't think I'd be much help to you.'

'It's best you stay here so you can keep the company informed and can tell Brunskill what's happening if he gets back with the posse.'

'I'll do that. Good luck.'

The mare was full of feed and energy and might have bucked if the rider had not held up her head and kept her moving. By the time she reached the back of the hotel though, the nervous tension was gone from her movements and she was beginning to relax.

'Chris.' The call came from an

upstairs window of the hotel. The guard looked up to see Ellen leaning from the window. 'Are you going for a ride?'

'Just having a look around.'

'Would you like some company? I have arranged to hire a horse from the livery stable. I'm going mad being stuck here. Could you wait for me?'

At any other time it would have been hard for him to resist the girl's offer but Chris had a strong sense of foreboding about what he was about to do. Trying not to sound too ungracious, he called back: 'Where I'm going isn't going to be very pleasant riding and I'm in a bit of a hurry. If you are still keen when I get back, we can have a nice ride somewhere else. I'm sorry but I have to go right now. I'll see you later.'

'Enjoy your ride.' There was a hint of frost in Ellen's voice.

If he heard it the guard seemed unaffected, for already his mind was on the tracks leading into the brush and up the rocky hill behind the town.

Dwyer was menace personified as he stood over the two bound and gagged prisoners at his feet. He was bluffing as he said: 'Now, Robert E. Grant, I have you at last. Nobody double-crosses Colonel Dwyer and lives. How smart do you feel now?'

The two prisoners, faces pale and eyes wide in terror looked at each other and made grunting noises behind their gags.

'I forgot,' Dwyer told them. 'You can't speak.' He nodded to Carrenza.

The Mexican drew a large Bowie knife from his belt and advanced on the two cowering prisoners. He cut away both gags in turn although he accidentally nicked Wilmot's cheek in the process. Wilmot went almost rigid with fear.

The colonel smiled and continued his game of bluff, hoping that the man he sought would reveal himself. He knew that Jones might well have been the elusive Grant but was not prepared to consider that situation until he had ruled out the other two.

'Jones talked before he died. I know that he was not Grant. It was one of you. Now which one of you miserable pigs is Robert E. Grant, the thief?'

Horace looked at Wilmot and said, 'He is.'

The accused man was nearly speechless with terror but eventually croaked. 'He's lying — he's Grant.'

For the first time for several days Dwyer was beginning to enjoy himself. He would soon find out the truth. But first he had an easier question. There was the matter of his cousin's death. 'Do you know the name of the shotgun guard on the coach?'

Both prisoners were keen to ingratiate themselves but Horace answered first. 'Sure do. He's a new man called Chris Unwin.'

'Was he at the saloon last night?'

This time Wilmot answered first. He remembered seeing the revolutionary with his bandaged head. 'No. He was probably down at the stage company office.'

'I can tell you what he looks like,' Horace volunteered. 'Maybe we can do a deal?'

'I know you will tell me what he looks like eventually and you can forget about any deals. All I needed was a name.'

'But the law's out after you,' Wilmot argued. 'You just can't walk into a town and grab him like you did us. I might be able to lure him out to where you can get him more easily.'

'The law is after Colonel Miguel Dwyer from Mexico. It is not after Mike Dyer, an Anglo rancher from New Mexico. I can come and go as I please. I would not trust either of you treacherous swine and all you have done is to convince me that one of you is Robert E. Grant. My man Carrenza has often seen the handiwork of the Apaches and is very good at interrogating prisoners. We will soon find out which one of you cheated me.'

'What happens to the one that ain't Grant?' A note of hope crept into Horace's voice.

Dwyer smiled. He was enjoying himself. 'He dies but probably less painfully than the other. We are in an isolated place, a long way from trails or people who might interfere. I am really going to enjoy this but I doubt that either of you will. Nobody is going to hear any scream.'

Wilmot groaned and fainted.

Distracted by the sound, Horace looked sideways to see Carrenza honing his knife on a small whetstone. He wished that he too could faint.

★ ★ ★

Ellen urged her hired mount through the brush following the tracks left by Chris and the others. From helping her father on the ranch she had acquired the necessary skill to track cattle in the brush and had no trouble following the horses.

At first she had been annoyed that Chris had left her behind but then, after talking to Amos, she realized that his mission was far more dangerous than his casual manner had suggested. The guard had a good half-hour start on her but Ellen had a clearer path to follow. The Mexicans had been forced to flounder around in darkness and had covered a lot of unnecessary ground. But in daylight it was possible to see how the lie of the land dictated where people could ride, so short cuts were easier to take even if any gains were gradual. Though feeling impatient and more than a little worried, she forced herself to let the horse make its own pace. It was a town animal that was past its prime and not very sure-footed. If the horse fell it could injure her, or itself, or possibly both of them and she would be no help to Chris then.

The guard was only half a mile ahead of Ellen when his horse suddenly picked up speed and looked eagerly ahead as though keen to catch up with the animals it was following. He knew that his quarry was close. Unsure whether the roan mare might neigh, he dismounted, hitched her securely to a nearby tree and went forward on foot. Picking his way among boulders, cactus and mesquite, Chris was aware of his vulnerability to ambush and could only hope that those he was following would not be expecting trouble.

The horse tracks led up a low but steep ridge; he was almost at the crest when a murmur of voices came from just beyond it. The guard paused for a few moments and listened. Though he could not hear the words, the tone of voice was conversational. He had not been detected.

With his carbine levelled ahead of him, his thumb on the hammer and finger on the trigger, he inched his way forward, alert for small, brittle twigs that would crack if he trod on them or even brushed against them.

★ ★ ★

Dwyer walked over to where Wilmot was lying and kicked him awake. He could see that Larry was the weaker of the two. 'Wake up, you miserable toad. I want to talk to you.'

'Don't kill me,' Wilmot pleaded. 'I don't know anything about this Grant character. It's not me.'

'He's got you dead to rights, Larry,' Horace said desperately. 'There's no point in us both getting tortured to death. For God's sake admit it.'

Dwyer was beginning to enjoy the situation and smiled. He kicked Horace in the ribs. 'Be quiet. There will be plenty of time for you to talk later before we cut out your tongue.' Then, turning to Carrenza he said, 'Which do you think we should start on?'

'It does not matter. The result will be

193

the same. Both will admit to being Robert E. Grant before I finish with them and one will be the right one.'

★　★　★

Chris had crept up the reverse slope of the ridge and peered through a crack between two boulders. He could hear the voices and knew that the men he sought were very close. His view was limited but he saw Horace and Wilmot on the ground and the legs of one of their captors. Where were the others? He knew he had been tracking at least three men. Then he heard two men debating which prisoner they should first start torturing. The voices accounted for two enemies but he could not attempt any sort of a rescue until he knew the whereabouts of the third.

Three-to-one odds in a gunfight were not good. The guard knew that he had a good chance of killing his first target but with the element of surprise gone, the remaining pair would present greater danger, specially as he could not locate the third man.

Cautiously he moved sideways seeking a better vantage point. Then he heard a faint sound coming from the brush behind him.

17

Turning quickly, Chris saw the tops of some bushes moving. Ominously too, those bushes were not tall enough to conceal a fully grown man. Whoever was approaching seemed to be crouching as though stalking him. He lined his Winchester's sights on a point about eighteen inches from where the moving bush tops betrayed the approaching person. A few more steps and each would be visible to the other.

The temptation to get in the first shot was a strong one but he had never been one to shoot before identifying his target. His shot would warn the men on the other side of the ridge but the alternative was to take a bullet. The guard had fully cocked his rifle and was taking up pressure on the trigger when the newcomer stepped into view.

He found his sights lined on the frilly

front of Ellen's pink blouse.

Shocked, he took his finger from the trigger and raised the rifle muzzle skywards.

'Chris,' he heard the girl say.

Luckily Ellen's voice was soft but he still feared that the sound might carry to Dwyer and his men. Frantically he signalled for silence with a finger to his lips.

Ellen looked puzzled but made no sound. He crept back to her.

'I damn near shot you. What are you doing here?'

'I thought you might need some help. I brought my gun along.'

'Any other time I'd be pleased to see you but there's at least two, maybe three *pistoleros* just over that rise and anything is likely to happen. You can help most by going back to the horses and holding them ready.'

'Another gun would be handy,' Ellen argued. 'I've backed you up before.'

'I know you have. But I would never

forgive myself if anything happened to you. If things go wrong I have to concentrate on Dwyer's men and I can't do that if I'm worrying about you. Please go back to the horses. I need you there in case I have to get out in a hurry. If you hear shooting, don't come to me. I'll come to you.'

'Don't you trust me? Do you think I'll panic and let you down?' Pain and anger came through in her voice.

'Ellen,' he said gently, 'You're a very special person. I know I can always trust you. So please trust my judgement now. We haven't known each other long but I've never met a girl like you. If anything happened to you I'd regret it for the rest of my life. Now, please — wait for me with the horses.'

'I think you are going about this the wrong way, Chris, but to please you I'll do as you ask. You be very careful and don't go getting yourself killed.'

* * *

Carrenza hauled Wilmot into a sitting position, dragged him against the twisted trunk of a gnarled cedar and called to Morillo: 'Get me another rope. This pig will start jumping around when I start on him. I'll need to tie him to this tree.'

'You have the wrong man,' the prisoner protested. 'You don't want me.'

'You don't want me either,' Horace yelled. 'You have the one you're after. Let me go. You have Larry. There's no need to stay around here.'

Dwyer contradicted him. 'You are forgetting about the death of my cousin Francisco. When we are finished here I am going after a certain shotgun guard named Unwin. I want people to know that a border is no protection for my enemies.'

'I could help you trap Unwin,' Wilmot volunteered.

'So could I,' Horace shouted.

'I would not trust either of you snakes.' Dwyer's voice dripped with contempt. 'Both of you would betray your own mothers if it suited you.' He turned to Carrenza. 'Your knife.'

With the gleaming blade in his hand, the colonel reached down and grabbed Horace by the ear. Driving the point through the middle, he cut upwards until the knife came free and his screaming victim was left with a long slit in the ear. 'Hurts — doesn't it? Now you know how my ear feels.'

'I didn't shoot you,' Horace groaned.

'You were there. Now we will see how your friend likes it.'

'No-o-o-o,' Wilmot howled in helpless protest as Dwyer grabbed his ear.

'If you wriggle I might cut the whole ear off,' the colonel warned.

'It does not matter if you do, Colonel,' Carrenza said casually. 'Eventually I will cut off both ears anyway.'

Chris had seen enough. Although he could not see all three revolutionaries, he jumped to his feet and snapped the carbine to his shoulder.

Morillo was the closest and he

reacted swiftly as he saw the rifleman on the high ground above him. He dropped the lariat he was carrying, shouted a warning and reached for his big Smith & Wesson revolver.

Swinging his rifle muzzle around, the guard fired. He knew immediately that he had over compensated for the downhill angle: the bullet that should have hit Morillo in the chest knocked his left leg from under him. As the man toppled, Chris sought his next opponent.

A gun blasted and a bullet fanned the air over his shoulder as Dwyer brought his gun into play. The guard snapped a shot back in reply but his target had already dived sideways.

Carrenza's weapon boomed then and a bullet whined off the boulder that partly sheltered Chris.

The captives wasted no time in getting out of the line of fire. Wilmot rolled sideways completely over Horace's body so that the latter shielded him from the flying lead. But two could play that game and Horace immediately rolled over Wilmot. A startled gasp broke from his lips as he found himself falling into a ditch, but the minor mishap proved to be a blessing in disguise because he found himself away from the path of stray bullets. Before he could fully appreciate his good fortune though, his terrified fellow prisoner crashed on top of him.

Dropping to the ground, Chris tried another shot at Dwyer, but a near miss from one of the other Mexicans threw dirt in his face as he fired and once more his bullet went astray. He was jacking another cartridge into the rifle when Carrenza gave a bellow and charged at him. Ignoring the other two gunmen the guard swung the muzzle of his Winchester at the oncoming man and squeezed the trigger. The bullet spun Carrenza around and the gun flew from his hand as he toppled forward. Immediately the shooter was looking for his next target.

A near miss from Morillo served

notice that the wounded man was still in the fight. He was lying in the open at the foot of the rise and was firing calmly at his attacker.

The situation was now a critical one for Chris. He had scored two hits but had only knocked one enemy out of the fight. Return shots were coming in from two different angles. Aware that Dwyer was the more dangerous of his enemies, he decided to concentrate on him, but the colonel had already sought a more sheltered position in the rocks and brush beyond the clearing.

Peering around the edge of a rock to shoot at Dwyer, the guard saw that Carrenza, though badly hit, was not dead and was crawling towards the six-gun he had dropped, leaving a bloody trail behind him. After firing the eleven shots in his carbine there was little time to reload it. While trying to keep the others busy by firing shots with his Colt, Chris used his left hand to slip cartridges through the carbine's loading port. The process was slow and awkward but he could not afford to be caught with an empty weapon. He decided to ignore Carrenza, gambling that the man was too badly wounded to shoot well.

Morillo had emptied his gun and was frantically reloading while Dwyer kept the guard busy by trying to angle shots around the rock that sheltered him.

A stalemate had developed with neither side able to get a clear shot at the other. The two wounded men were not under good cover but the guard had to expose himself to Dwyer's gun to get a shot at either of them. The pair, in turn, prevented him from getting a good shot at their leader.

Between shots Chris silently cursed Horace and Wilmot. If it were not for their presence he would be able to retreat and rely on the law to track down the revolutionaries. Hampered by two wounded men, Dwyer would have trouble evading a posse. The temptation came to abandon the fight, but to do so would spell certain death for the two captives.

A brief lull occurred as both sides paused to reload their weapons. Aware that neither of the wounded men was likely to attempt to rush him, the guard knew that Dwyer would have to change his position considerably before he posed any greater threat. His ears straining to catch the slightest sound, he breathed more easily when he snapped shut the loading gate on his Colt and slipped the fully loaded weapon back in its holster.

A call in Spanish came from Dwyer's position. As Chris did not speak the language he had no idea of what it said, but he knew that it signalled another move from his adversaries. Then bullets began bouncing off the sheltering rocks or kicking up loose dirt from the crest of the ridge. All were coming from where he knew Dwyer to be and the new tactic puzzled him for a while. The colonel was unlikely to empty his own gun if he intended a direct, frontal attack. Chris was sure then that one of the wounded men was making some sort of move, but he could not hear anyone approaching his position. If either wounded man could walk at all he could not move silently.

The guard was not to know that, slowly and painfully, Carrenza was dragging himself towards the ditch where the two prisoners were cowering. Dwyer's shouted orders had been for him to kill them both.

18

From the bottom of the ditch Horace whispered to Wilmot, 'Have a look and see what's happening.'

'You have a look,' his fellow captive said.

'I can't — you're lyin' on top of me.'

'You're crazy if you think I'm going to stick my head up. Those Mexicans have forgotten us and I don't intend reminding them that we're still here. I'm not showing myself until Unwin calls out that it is safe.'

'At least you could try doing something useful. What about trying to bite through my ropes?'

'I'm staying here. You can get up and run if you want to but don't blame me if you get shot. And you can bite through your own ropes too.'

'How in the hell can I? My hands are tied behind my back. You're being very selfish about this, Larry. The odds against Unwin are three to one. What do you think is going to happen to us when he gets killed?'

Wilmot wriggled around to get his feet under him. 'I'm not waiting around to find out,' he announced. 'I can still run and I intend doing that as soon as I'm out of this hole. Feel free to do the same but don't run where I'm going. We need them to split up.'

This news disturbed Horace greatly. He knew that with the element of surprise, Wilmot might just escape to the brush but he would emerge some time later and his attempt would be expected. With his hands bound, minus his boots, with rocks and cactus underfoot, he was unlikely to outrun a bullet.

Wilmot struggled to his knees but as his eyes came over the edge of the ditch, he gave a blood-curdling shriek of unadulterated fear.

Barely six feet away a blood-spattered Carrenza was struggling along the ground towards him with determination in his face and a six-gun in his hand.

Chris heard the scream and two shots. He tried to look around the boulder but a near miss sprayed his face with tiny pieces of rock and sent him reeling back under cover. So much for Horace and Wilmot, he thought.

A gun fired again and he heard faltering footsteps in the gravel on the other side of the boulder that sheltered him. At least one attacker was very close. He knew that the man was wounded but did not know how severely. However, he felt that it was safer to take the initiative than to give the Mexicans time to follow the plan they were undoubtedly using.

Transferring the rifle to his left hand, Chris drew and cocked his Colt. He had to remove the closest threat and be back under cover before Dwyer could react with covering fire.

The scraping of boots on the gravel betrayed the position of the man close to him. For all the guard knew, the colonel was waiting for him to react in the manner he was planning, but he staked everything on surprise.

Two quick strides took him around the rock, and there, almost in touching distance, was a Mexican propped against the boulder to ease a wounded leg. The man had a gun in his hand but, caught by surprise, was fatally slow in lining up his target.

Chris triggered two quick shots. The first one sent his man reeling backwards and the second knocked him down. The way his body rolled back down the slope was a sure indication that Dwyer's man was no longer a problem.

He looked around for the colonel and saw movement in the brush across the small clearing. Even as he snapped a shot at the fleeting target, a gun snarled again from the direction taken by the wounded Carrenza. He could not see the man but wasted no time in jumping back under cover. A bullet from Dwyer buzzed past him as he did so.

The unseen gunman fired again but Chris had no idea where his shots were landing.

Peering through a crack between two boulders, Chris saw violent movement at the edge of the brush about fifty yards away. Though partly screened by low greasewood he saw the Mexicans' three horses hitched to trees. They had been well trained but were shuffling nervously at every shot. It would not take much to frighten them into breaking their bridles: an idea quickly formed in his mind.

Chris sighted carefully through the gap between the rocks and planted a rifle bullet into the tree trunk within inches of a tethered horse's face. Possibly stung by a piece of displaced bark and thoroughly frightened, the horse snorted, pulled back and broke its bridle. As it did so it backed into the animal tied near it. This caused the second horse to panic. Eyes rolling in fright, the bay pony threw itself sideways snapping its headstall in the process. The bit snagged on the pony's teeth, causing another flurry of panicked activity. By the time the bridle slipped free the contagious fear had infected the third animal. Seconds later the three startled horses were smashing their way through the brush, leaving their former riders behind.

Dwyer cursed but could do nothing. Being left afoot was bad enough but his rifle was also on the saddle of his runaway mount. He had seen Morillo cut down and no longer knew what had happened to Carrenza, but he suspected that he had died of his wound. There had been a couple of stray shots from the direction Carrenza had taken but, from his present position, the colonel could not see his man or where the prisoners had taken refuge. The situation had become confused but the guard was rapidly gaining control. He needed time to think. 'You, out there,' he called. 'Who are you? Are you the law?'

'No, but I'll have to do until it comes along.'

'I'm Colonel Dwyer and I can call on a hundred men. Don't bite off more than you can chew. Back away now and save your life.'

'Anyone you can call on is either dead in Mexico, or heading there as fast as they can go. Throw out your gun because if you don't I'll probably have to kill you.'

'If you're not a lawman why do you have to kill me? Can't we do a deal?'

'I'm after you because I work for Rutherford coaches. Your men killed a couple of ours and now you've killed three of our passengers. As a shotgun guard I feel partly responsible for those people. The only deal I'm prepared to make is to let you surrender and take your chances with the law.'

Dwyer called back: 'You say you are a guard. Is your name Unwin?'

'That's right. How did you know?'

'I made it my business to find out. I intend to kill you. If you have any sense you will start running now, because when I come over there you will die.'

'Come any time you feel like it. I'll be waiting.'

That was just the news that Dwyer wanted to hear. He wanted to put his opponent on the defensive. He wanted him to be keyed up and expecting an attack. But the colonel had other plans.

19

Wilmot could not believe his luck. One moment he had been staring into the muzzle of Carrenza's gun. Then a shot came from the brush behind him and the wounded revolutionary's head jerked violently under the impact of a bullet. A split second later another shot kicked up dirt inches from the fallen man's head.

Ellen emerged from the brush, a smoking gun in her hand.

'Miss Ellen, what are you doing here?'

'There's no time for talking, Larry. We have to help Chris.'

Horace somehow lurched to his feet throwing Wilmot aside as he went. 'Nice work, Miss Ellen — you're an angel. If you can get my hands loose, I can get that *bandido*'s gun and help out. It sounds like Chris is keeping

Dwyer busy but we don't know for how long. There's a knife on that dead *hombre's* belt. Get it quick and cut me loose. Hurry — he won't bite you.'

Gingerly the girl stepped across the ditch and nervously plucked the knife from its sheath. Horace turned so she could get at his bonds.

'You had better throw another shot in Dwyer's direction. Just to keep him guessing.'

Because of the brush Ellen could not really see where the colonel was but fired in his general direction before applying the razor-sharp knife to Horace's bonds. As soon as the ropes fell away he hopped awkwardly across to the fallen Mexican and snatched up his revolver. Seconds later he had removed the dead man's cartridge belt and was rapidly replacing the fired shots in the revolver's chamber. He was wondering about the Mexican's boot size when Wilmot complained.

'What about me?' he whined. 'Isn't anyone going to cut me free?'

Leaving Horace to keep watch, Ellen took the knife and soon severed Wilmot's bonds. Without waiting for the others he scampered into the brush, realized that he did not know where he was going and halted again, uncertainly.

Horace shouted. 'Chris — we're here in the brush somewhere on your left. We have a couple of extra guns. How many are left?'

The guard had been sure that his two former passengers were dead, but there was no mistaking Horace's rasping voice. He thought for a moment, then called back, 'There's only Dwyer left. Be careful. He could be somewhere in range of you.'

But Chris was wrong.

Dwyer had silently stolen away. He had no intention of staying where he was. Hoping that his antagonist had been sitting tight and expecting an attack, he had set out on the tracks of the runaway horses. If he was lucky they would not have travelled far. The fright would not stay with them for long. The chance existed that he could find them and escape while the guard waited for an attack that would not come. He was amazed and greatly disappointed to hear Horace's voice, but the colonel decided that self-preservation was the most important task before him. Revenge would have to wait. He promised himself, though, that at some later date he would return and track down those of his enemies who had destroyed his plans.

The horse tracks were easy to follow and occasionally he heard the animals breaking through the brush in the distance. Hoping to find them at the first patch of good grass, the colonel hurried away from the scene of the fight.

Chris was not happy when he saw Ellen with Horace and Wilmot emerging from the brush nearby. 'You were supposed to be looking after the horses,' he said accusingly.

Ellen's chin went up and she said defiantly, 'Nobody died and left you boss, Chris Unwin. I thought it more important to help you but on the way I had to divert to do something that you had failed to do, namely to save Larry and Horace.'

'That's right,' Horace agreed. 'If it hadn't been for Miss Ellen, we would both be dead.'

'I'm sorry, Ellen. I was worried that you might get hurt. You did great and I know I sounded like a jackass. I'm sorry.'

'You should be too,' Wilmot snapped. 'We're alive because of Miss Ellen.'

'No, you're not,' the girl corrected. 'You're alive because Chris tracked down those men and stopped them killing you. It was a joint effort and too much for one man.'

Horace brought them back to reality. 'I'm not sure who's sidin' with who here but I reckon we should be worryin' about Dwyer. He's out there in the brush somewhere and he hasn't fired for quite a while. Either he's high-tailed it out of here or he's creepin' up on us while we argue about who did what. Standin' round here in a bunch is givin' him too many easy targets.'

Dwyer, however, had lost interest in his late adversaries. Not far ahead he heard horses coming through the brush. At first he thought that the runaways had changed direction. Then, all too close, he heard men talking. Even as he drew his gun, a man on a tall black horse came around the side of a massive boulder. A silver star stood out against the black background of the man's vest.

The horse shied as Dwyer launched himself at it. He was lucky because he caught the near-side rein with his left hand. The gun in his right hand swung in an arc, caught the startled rider in the face and knocked him from the saddle. Before Brunskill really knew what was happening he was lying dazed on the ground and Dwyer had vaulted on to his horse. He was thirty yards away before the rest of the posse knew what had happened. One man dismounted to aid the sheriff but the others yelled and spurred their mounts after his attacker.

The colonel's first task was to make good his escape. He was not fussy where he went as long as he shook off the riders behind him. One man had already tried a shot at him but given the colonel's speed and the nature of the country, the bullet was wasted.

Chris and the others heard the shot and seconds later hoofbeats and smashing bushes warned that someone was coming through the brush with no small degree of urgency.

'Sounds like trouble headed this way,' Chris said. 'Everyone get under cover.' As he spoke he looked for a likely boulder, caught Ellen by the arm and pushed her behind it. 'Stay there.'

Wilmot sought shelter behind the too-narrow trunk of a gnarled cedar but Horace, on bootless, sore feet, was a little on the slow side as he looked about for likely protection. Chris ran to his side. 'Get down in the mesquite.'

Then the black horse came bursting from the trees and into the clearing where they stood. Low branches had swept Dwyer's hat from his head but there was no mistaking the telltale bandage around it. His concentration had been on the pursuers and momentarily he was surprised to find himself where he was. But suddenly the colonel saw two of his enemies standing almost directly in his path. Even before he drew his gun he had steered his mount straight at Chris.

The space between them diminished rapidly; both men raised and cocked their weapons.

The guard forced himself to ignore the onrushing horse. He knew that few horses would deliberately run over a man. Instead he carefully aimed at the centre of the colonel's striped shirt.

Dwyer fired first and though he missed his target, the shot was not wasted. The excited horse shied sideways as the gun fired. The bullet that

Chris had aimed so carefully flew harmlessly past.

Both men were now only a couple of yards apart, a range where missing was unlikely.

The guard fired first and quickly jumped sideways to avoid being run down by the animal that seemed to be fleeing blindly with no guidance from its rider.

Dwyer's gun went off but none of the onlookers knew where the bullet went. Chris's shot had taken effect. The colonel tumbled from the saddle, hit the ground in a cloud of dust and rolled awkwardly.

Somewhere behind Chris a gun fired rapidly. The guard felt the wind of the passing bullets and saw Dwyer's body jerk as at least one of the shots struck home. A couple of others kicked up dirt around the fallen man.

'I got him!' Wilmot shouted in triumph and waved the now-empty gun he had taken from Morillo's corpse.

'You damn near got me too,' Chris

said angrily. He saw the last flicker of life drain from Dwyer's body.

'I killed him — I'm claiming the reward.' Wilmot's excitement grew.

'You miserable sonofabitch.' Horace's words expressed his contempt. 'There was no reward on this *hombre*. But I'll make sure that you get your reward. Wherever I go I'll spread the story of what a great gunfighter you are. People will know you as the man who killed the toughest *pistolero* ever to come out of Mexico. Then every crazy, would-be gunfighter will be looking to challenge you. I'll make sure you're famous, Larry, but you will have a hard time trying to enjoy your new reputation.'

20

The posse, with Sheriff Brunskill riding behind one of its members, arrived before the gunsmoke had blown away. Still partly dazed by the blow Dwyer had given him, the lawman looked about the scene and muttered, 'What in the hell has been going on here?'

'We got the ones you were after,' Horace said. 'The ones that stopped our coach and killed John Jones.'

Ellen pointed to Dwyer's body. 'The army is after that man. He's a revolutionary from Mexico.'

Wilmot chimed in: 'They were going to kill us.'

Brunskill slipped from his horse's rump and winced as the landing jarred his aching head. 'Now just hold on a minute. One at a time, tell me what happened. Ladies first.'

By the time all had recounted their

versions of the events the sheriff had the complete picture in his mind. 'There's still one thing that's puzzling me,' he said slowly. 'Why was a Mexican revolutionary so dead set on chasing you folks?'

Chris answered, 'He was taken down by a man calling himself Robert E. Grant. This character swindled Dwyer, thinking that the colonel would not be able to do anything about it. Dwyer was sure he was on our coach from Muddy Creek and that's why he tried to stop us. He and his men followed us to Holford but lured you away after they killed Jones. Then they grabbed Horace and Larry and brought them here to kill them. Miss Fletcher and I managed to prevent that. Dwyer might have escaped if he hadn't run into you.'

The sheriff explained: 'I've led a lot of posses around this district and when I lose a trail, I make sure that I've combed the area thoroughly before heading back to town. These aren't the first criminals who have tried to hide here. We heard shooting, so we were heading straight for this place when Dwyer jumped me. By the way, which one of you gents is this Robert E. Grant?'

'Not me,' Wilmot announced.

'Wasn't me neither,' Horace said emphatically. 'Either Dwyer got things wrong or it was Jones. The trouble was that he thought it was one of us. Maybe Jones told him that in the hope that he wouldn't kill him. Did this Grant fella break any laws?'

The sheriff shook his head and wished he had not. It was still aching. 'As far as I can see he hasn't broken any of our laws, but then we don't really know what he did. There might be some minor technicality somewhere but unless I receive a solid complaint, I'm not after this Grant character.'

Suddenly Wilmot had a flash of inspiration. 'Did it ever occur to anyone that Grant might not have been a passenger? What about Chris here, or Amos?'

With great difficulty the guard refrained from grabbing his accuser by the shirtfront. Instead he muttered angrily, 'If you say that again, Larry, I am going to get violent with you and do something that I know you won't like.'

'You can't talk to me like that. I'm a paying customer of your coach line and you should be showing me some respect. I have good grounds for my suspicions. You have only recently joined the coach line. What did you do before that?'

Ellen intervened at this point. 'Both of you, simmer down. It's all over and this Grant person is not important. Let's stop this silly arguing and work out how we are all getting back to town.'

'There are three loose horses out in the brush,' Chris said. 'It shouldn't be too hard for a rider to round them up. Their bridles are over there in the brush. We can patch them up enough to get them back to Holford.'

★ ★ ★

The following day the Rutherford Coach Line resumed operations but Chris started work a bit earlier than Amos. He knocked on Ellen's door. When she opened it she bore little resemblance to the girl who had shared their recent adventures. If she had looked a little bedraggled when they returned to Holford she was a different person now, so beautiful and carefully groomed. For a moment he thought that he was being far too ambitious. Ladies like that did not marry ordinary men like him. But the sudden welcoming smile and sparkle in her eyes reassured him. He explained his presence nervously. 'Er — I thought you might need someone to carry your bag to the coach.'

'Does the coach line extend this service to all its passengers?'

'Only the pretty ones who have climbed mountains and shot it out with Mexican bandits.'

'So that excludes Horace and Larry. Is either of them coming back to Muddy Creek?'

'I hope not. They won't be with us on this trip anyway. I don't want to see either of them again.'

'I thought Horace was nice,' Ellen said as she passed her bag to Chris and closed the door of the hotel room behind her.

'Horace was the cause of all our trouble,' he told her. 'He was Robert E. Grant.'

A tinge of disbelief was in Ellen's voice. 'Are you sure?'

'I'm sure. Horace had worked with a buffalo-shooting outfit and could get his hands on obsolete 50/70 ammunition that the army was giving free to the shooters. He sold it to Dwyer's man along with a load of gravel in some of the boxes. He knew that the cartridges would fit the Mexican carbines but were really too strong for them. Remember, up on the mountain, when he gave that carbine and ammunition to Wilmot? Normally that rifle would be worth its weight in gold to folks in our situation but Horace was not game to fire it. That's why he gave it away.'

'Are you certain of this?'

'I tackled Horace last night and he admitted it. He told me the whole story. He had no idea that his little swindle would cause the loss of life that it did but was happy to blame Jones or Wilmot for it. He lives on his wits and is smart enough to know that a man with a cheerful personality is forgiven much. But, deep down, he's pretty much like Wilmot.'

'Maggie and I were sure that Larry was Grant. What about Horace's threat to give him a false reputation as a gunslinger?'

'I persuaded him to drop that idea. I reminded him of the deaths he had already caused and that if anything happened to Larry, I would personally track him down and shoot him like a mad dog.'

Ellen looked at him in disbelief. 'You wouldn't do that?'

'He thinks I would.'

A small hand slipped inside Chris's

free arm. The guard looked down to an upturned, smiling face. One lingering kiss seemed scarcely enough but both knew that they could not keep Amos waiting.

The driver was glowering from his seat and the team was impatient to go when the guard helped Ellen into the coach and closed the door. 'Get that smile off your face, young fella,' he growled as Chris climbed up beside him. 'You're grinning like a goat on a trash heap. I don't know how someone like you can snare a nice girl like that. You must be mighty lucky.'

The guard laughed. 'Just this once, Amos, I'll agree with you.'

'As long as you don't make a habit of it,' the driver muttered.

We do hope that you have enjoyed reading this large print book.

Did you know that all of our titles are available for purchase?

We publish a wide range of high quality large print books including:
Romances, Mysteries, Classics
General Fiction
Non Fiction and Westerns

Special interest titles available in large print are:
The Little Oxford Dictionary
Music Book, Song Book
Hymn Book, Service Book

Also available from us courtesy of Oxford University Press:
Young Readers' Dictionary
(large print edition)
Young Readers' Thesaurus
(large print edition)

For further information or a free brochure, please contact us at:
Ulverscroft Large Print Books Ltd.,
The Green, Bradgate Road, Anstey,
Leicester, LE7 7FU, England.
Tel: (00 44) **0116 236 4325**
Fax: (00 44) **0116 234 0205**

VALLEY OF THE GUNS

Rick Dalmas

Zack Clay is looking for a quiet life, but he hasn't reckoned on range-grabbers Dutch Haas and Burt Helidon bringing in sundry gun-fighters to hassle him. Clay meets fists and boots with the same, gunsmoke with gunsmoke. In the end, they hang a badge on him. Then things really hot up in Benbow. But the hustlers, gunslingers, the wild trailmen and townsmen who put dollars before citizens all find that stubborn Zack Clay won't go down without a fight . . .